HUMBUG

LUCIANO MARANO

Crystal Lake Publishing
Where Stories Come Alive!

www.crystallakepub.com

Join the Crystal Lake community today
on our newsletter and Patreon!
https://linktr.ee/CrystalLakePublishing

Download our latest catalog here:
https://geni.us/CLPCatalog

ISBN: 978-1-968532-35-2

Cover Art:
Blaine Daigle | blainedaigle.com

Layout:
Jacque Day | jacqueday.com

Follow us on Amazon:

WELCOME
TO ANOTHER

CRYSTAL LAKE PUBLISHING
CREATION

Join today at www.crystallakepub.com & www.patreon.com/CLP

CONTENTS

For Liane: my wife, best friend, and favorite person.
I will hold you close in a thankful heart.

PREFACE

Is *A Christmas Carol* the most famous ghost story ever written? Washington Irving's "The Legend of Sleepy Hollow" might come close, but I think it probably is. Consider that for a moment: the most popular ghost story in the world (well, the English-speaking world) for the better part of the last two centuries is not only a Christmas tale, but one which features a famously optimistic ending. Who says ours is a cynical age?

I began working on the story that would become *Humbug* in December 2023, exactly one hundred eighty years after Charles Dickens first published the iconic tale that was its inspiration and model. Funny enough, it was while my wife and I were enjoying our annual screening of *The Muppet Christmas Carol* that I first contemplated the idea of writing a modern, more transgressive version of the story. Something about an abundance of wholesome cheer always turns me into a contrarian...

Takes a large drink of whiskey and turns pointedly away from deeper self-examination

As I was saying, there have been scores of homages and adaptations of the novella, but there had been no contemporary version, I thought, quite dark enough to give modern audiences a sense of the shivering thrill I imagine was felt by initial readers. *A Christmas Carol is*, after all, subtitled: *Being a Ghost Story of Christmas.*

Familiarity breeds contempt, as they say, and somewhere along the line, what with all the puppets and cartoons and plays and TV specials, Bill Murray and Patrick Stewart, I think we became just a little too familiar with the story. Scrooge's redemption is the ultimate point of the narrative, but damned if I didn't want more fearsome ghosts in this ghost story—I wanted to make it once again equally hopeful *and scary*. So that's what I did (or tried to do).

I sincerely hope you enjoy my twisted take on Dickens's classic and want to thank you for making it a part of your holiday, whatever name you give the occasion, however you choose to celebrate. Now let us begin, shall we?

Here's a properly macabre ghost story for Christmas, and you only *think* you know what happens. Turn down the lights and check if your door is locked (not that it will help, I suspect). Tell me, is it cold where you are? Is it dark? Listen carefully. Can you hear that? If I didn't know better I'd say it almost sounds like the clinking of...*chains*. And I think they're getting closer. Are you alone tonight?

Are you sure?

Luciano Marano
Bainbridge Island, Washington
September 2025

THAT CORNY DICKENS CRAP (MARLEY'S GHOST)

Marley was dead.

The decorated, young police detective's beloved Harley Super Glide had superbly glided on a patch of black ice, straight into the path of an oncoming truck. Marley's helmet shattered like an eggshell, her skull quickly following suit, with her brain playing the part of yolk.

So, yeah, Marley Graves was definitely dead.

Living up to her name, as it were.

Certifiably deceased.

No longer of this Earth, you could say.

That, alone, would have been enough to make Detective Stewart "Scrooge" Caine hate Christmas. Hard and disagreeable a man though he famously was, Scrooge had genuinely cared for his partner. He believed in no kind of afterlife and entertained no possibility that such a tragic happening might be part of some unknowable design or deliberate plan at work in the universe. He had no patience for the concept of forgiveness. For Scrooge, the senseless premature death of his best (and only) friend would have been more than sufficient cause to ruin Christmas all on its own.

But there was actually much more behind his vitriolic hatred of the holiday.

It was just after 8 a.m. on Christmas Eve, and Detective Caine stood alone outside the conference room on the top floor of Seattle Police Department headquarters. A tall white man of about sixty, handsome and solidly built, though carrying a noticeable belly, he ran a hand through the thinning ash-gray remains of his hair, smoothing it back from his furrowed brow.

Scrooge wore a beige trench coat and rumpled suit. In warmer months he ditched the coat and would often loosen his tie, perhaps unbutton the collar of his shirt, but otherwise always looked exactly the same regardless of season or occasion. His narrowed eyes were a shade of blue so startlingly light they were almost clear, seemingly scoured clean by the many atrocities to which he'd been forced to bear witness.

Through a collection of snowman decals plastered on the windows, Scrooge saw curtains of rain falling onto the gloomy city outside. It was a particularly soggy and frigid winter in Seattle. The sun had yet to rise that morning, and the drastic temperature drop expected later would mean treacherous roads. He stuffed his hands into his coat pockets, fighting the urge to rip down the laughing cartoons. Or put his fists through the glass. Or both.

For as long as he could remember, Scrooge had *hated* Christmas.

Even before he was curtly summoned to HQ for an ominously early meeting with the Chief of Police, and a veritable murderer's row of civil and governmental muckety-mucks, all of them far more concerned with their tablets and cellphones than listening to the detective answer the questions they'd called him there to pose, Scrooge was *disgusted* by Christmas.

Even before the Christian festival celebrating the birth of Jesus became the same day on which his partner died in a horrific motorcycle accident, Scrooge *despised* Christmas.

Even before it was chosen as the annual occasion, now five years running, for a vicious serial killer known only as Humbug, a brilliant and sadistic psychopath, to slaughter an entire family for no discernible reason, Scrooge *loathed* December 25.

But even that hadn't been the true start of it.

Long before he was first saddled with the nickname Scrooge, a dubious honor bestowed initially by the more cynical members of the city's sensation-hungry media and later his own snickering colleagues, Detective Caine *abhorred* everything about the season.

Being totally honest, though, the nickname hadn't helped.

But it sure sold a lot of newspapers.

One particularly memorable headline from early in the Humbug investigation read "Scrooge & Marley Stumped by Ghosts of Christmas Past—and Present!" Another from the following year said, "MORE Murders: What the Dickens are Scrooge & Marley doing to catch Seattle's Xmas Killer?" And finally, from one year ago, with Marley dead less than twenty-four hours, "Humbug Christmas Carnage Continues! Scrooge Solo After Marley's Mishap!!"

The rest of the story was all too familiar. Yet another family was butchered in their home on Christmas Day. Another macabre holiday card left behind with yet another taunting message from the murderer.

Given such a situation, you couldn't really blame the press.

A cunning serial killer who murdered one family every year on Christmas? The press lost no time in christening their new favorite villain "Humbug."

Add to that a homicide detective named Marley, and her scowling quick-tempered old grump of a partner?

Scrooge. Yeah, it had almost been too easy.

The door of the conference room opened and a mousy civilian aide in an ugly Christmas sweater with an enormous smiling reindeer on it motioned Scrooge back inside. Seated around the long, shiny table were the topmost department brass and biggest political bigwigs in Seattle. Several F.B.I. consultants were also in attendance, their stony expressions eerily unreadable.

At the head, Chief Karen Woodard steepled her fingers above a pile of paperwork. A striking dark-skinned woman of an age not immediately obvious, the breast of her dress uniform overburdened with medals, she leveled her gaze onto Scrooge like the rifle sights of a firing squad resigned to the unpleasant task ahead.

"Detective," she said, "thanks for your patience. Having listened to your report and discussed the situation, let me begin by saying that everyone has nothing but respect for you and a sincere appreciation for your notable career. Considering your impressive arrest record, there can be no doubt you are an incredible asset to this—"

"If it's all the same, Chief," Scrooge said, "I'd just as soon you stop feeling me up and get straight to the screwing."

"Excuse me?"

"Dress it up however you like. But we all know I'm leaving this room with my lipstick smeared and reputation tarnished. So, go ahead, do me already."

"That is exactly what I'm talking about," said Frank Murray. The prissy bald man seated four chairs to the left of Chief Woodard slammed his impeccably manicured fist onto the table. "The guy is an embarrassment. He can't even pretend to take this review seriously. How are we supposed to believe him capable of managing the task force of a complex criminal investigation?"

Visions danced in Scrooge's head of severed feet stuffed into stockings and hung carefully over a cheerfully blazing fireplace; the soft, red fabric so thoroughly soaked with blood they looked black. Candy canes sucked sharp, their pointy ends stabbed into wide terrified eyeballs. Blood tended to pool inside a dead body at the lowest point—the head, say, if a person had been suspended upside down. If they'd been hung by their feet, for instance, with strands of twinkling lights. His attention kept straying back to the aide's sweater; the blank idiotic stare of the reindeer. And for a moment, Scrooge did not realize he'd spoken.

"Tell the mayor that not all the victims were registered voters. That should make him feel better."

"You've got some nerve making comments like that at a time like this," Frank Murray's delicate fingers busily straightened his necktie. "And you can be sure that when the mayor hears about your attitude, you'll be lucky to land a job as a crossing guard in this city."

"Gentlemen!" Chief Woodard's tone silenced the room and her glare made the bald man's fingers leap to smooth his pocket square.

"Mr. Murray, I'll remind you this is *my* police department. I'll handle matters of personnel assignments as I see fit. And if the mayor doesn't like it, he damn well knows how to reach me."

Turning to Scrooge, she said, "As for you, Detective. Given your own evaluation of the case, which you just presented to us, can you honestly say that a change of leadership is unwarranted? I'll ask you plainly. Are you any closer to catching Humbug now than you were a year ago?"

"As I explained," Scrooge fought to keep his eyes off the aide's sweater, "we are exploring numerous potential leads and reviewing several promising suspects."

"Yes, well," Chief Woodard began gathering her papers, "be that as it may, we've decided to take a different tack."

"I see."

"You will be reassigned after the first of the year. For now, consider yourself on a leave of absence—with pay, of course. I'm sorry, but I have to do what I think is best for the public."

"Who's it going to be?" Scrooge asked. "The person taking over Humbug. Which of your precious little criminologist geeks is in line for my job? None of them have any guts, you know. All they know are *microfibers* and *behavior analysis*."

"I'm assigning Detective Alwyn."

"Bobby? Baby Face Bobby is the best you can do? First, you make me change the kid's diaper for a year, then you hand over my case to him?"

"Robert Alwyn has received nothing but stellar fitness reports from every officer he's served under. And I believe he's already learned a great deal more in his time working with you. He may be a young man, your partner, but he's—"

"He's not my partner," Scrooge said. "He was my responsibility, never my partner. My partner died one year ago. Her brains were smeared all over the highway, remember? I sure as hell do."

"Save it," Frank Murray said, pulling at the cuffs of his shirt. "We all know Marley was the smart one. She was the prodigy, the super cop. And if she couldn't solve this thing what the hell are you going to do? You were barely qualified to be that girl's chauffeur, *Scrooge.*"

"Don't call me that."

"Face it, you're a relic. Just another burnout leg-breaker holding on longer than he should for a slightly less pathetic pension."

Scrooge felt each heartbeat strike the back of his eyes. The reindeer seemed now to be looking directly at him—*laughing* at him. "I'll be glad to break more than just your legs, you fussy little shit, if you'd care to step outside."

Following several loud and colorful exclamations not entirely in keeping with the spirit of the season, the meeting was hastily concluded.

Scrooge stepped out of the elevator and stormed through the lobby, his attention on the front doors and street beyond—*escape*—but his path was blocked by a pale overweight man rushing in from the rain. Oliver Drood's messy black hair was dripping wet, and he was so intently focused on the stack of photographs he carried, glossy prints of a suburban bedroom streaked with blood, that he nearly tripped over his own feet, twice.

"Heads up, Drood." Scrooge shoved the man aside. "I'm walking here."

"I went to snap a double over on Mercer Island last night." Behind the thick, rain-flecked lenses of his glasses, Oliver's eyes were wide and bright, as if from too much caffeine. "Murder-suicide, probably. Look, Detective. Just look at how the husband managed to get himself out of bed and down the hallway. Remarkable, don't you think? I mean for him to have moved that far with his cock cut off? And his wife made an even bigger mess of herself downstairs in the kitchen. You want to see?"

Scrooge grunted noncommittally and moved around the photographer.

"I heard about your big meeting today," Oliver continued examining his pictures as he spoke. "Might I take a guess at the outcome?"

"You've got tinsel in your hair."

Oliver reached to remove the glittering strands tucked behind his ear. "Occupational hazard. It can be something of a chore, finding just the right angle from which to best shoot a scene. Guess I shouldn't even bother to wish you a Merry Christmas."

"I wouldn't."

"Humbug," Oliver shook his head. "Those vultures in the press can't be expected to understand what's happening because they aren't forced to look at the true face of the city. To live with it in our hearts every day, all year long."

"Take it up with Alwyn," Scrooge said, walking away. "He's the one who'll be living with it from now on."

"Don't worry, Detective," Oliver called after him, "everything will work out—you'll see! They'll beg you to come back. Nobody really appreciates anything until it's gone." He held up another picture from the Mercer Island crime scene. "Just ask this guy!"

Outside, Scrooge stood in the rain breathing deeply the cold wet air, knowing he was dangerously close to losing control and knowing full well what that might entail. What such lapses *had* entailed in times not-so-long past.

Warnings, reprimands, suspensions—his troubled reputation meant that when his previous partner retired, not many cops were lining up to work with Scrooge. But a cocky hotshot young lady with an advanced degree wasn't any more attractive as a potential partner for most men on the force. They'd made an unlikely alliance, Scrooge and Marley. One that proved shockingly effective and quickly racked up an enviable record.

Beauty and Beast.

Brains and Brawn.

The energy of youth and weight of experience.

Marley had been a great calming influence, too, always knowing exactly what to say to hold Scrooge back from indulging in his worst impulses. She'd also known when to cut him loose and exactly how far to let him go before yanking his collar again. With Marley gone, forced for the first time in a long time to think for himself, Scrooge felt his guts roil with an acidic blend of fury and fear.

He pushed the feeling aside as best he could, grinding his teeth loudly enough to be heard by the uniformed figures entering and leaving the building behind him. Recognizing Scrooge, those cops, without speaking, went far out of their way to give him a wide berth.

"It wasn't my idea." From beneath the awning of the adjacent building, Detective Robert "Bobby" Alwyn came forward holding two lidded cups of coffee. "I just want you to know that. They only came to me yesterday."

His hopelessly boyish face was only made more conspicuously youthful by the mustache he'd recently grown. A thin white man whose brown hair was buzzed militarily short, his large soulful eyes seemed to helplessly broadcast his every thought. He offered a cup to Scrooge, saying, "I'm really sorry."

Scrooge knocked the drink from his hand and walked away, leaving the younger man scurrying to follow.

"Please, don't be like that. I know you're mad, but I was hoping I could still get your advice on things as they come up. New developments, fresh evidence, stuff like that? And when I bring somebody in for an interrogation, I'd like you to be there with me. Nobody is better in the room than you, every cop in the city knows that."

"Yeah, sure." Scrooge stopped at his car, an old Ford Taurus more rust than red, and searched for his keys. "Everybody wants answers, but nobody wants to get their hands dirty asking the questions."

"Hey," Bobby put a hand on Scrooge's shoulder, "I'm sorry they took you off the case, but it wasn't my decision. I'm sorry that

Marley died, but that wasn't my fault. And I know this time of year is hard for you, but that's no excuse to keep treating me... Look, I tried to be a good partner, give you plenty of space and keep my mouth shut. Jesus Christ, why do you always have to be such an asshole, Scrooge?"

"Don't call me that." Turning slowly, keys in hand, Scrooge fought to keep his face blank. *Never let them see what you're thinking* was a tried-and-true tenet of Marley's, but one he'd yet to master. "And don't touch me again."

"My bad," Bobby backed away, hands raised. "Look, I have to go. There's a million things to do before...well, before tomorrow." An intense weariness passed across his eyes. "It's going to be rough."

"I'm certain you'll have it wrapped up in no time," Scrooge unlocked his car and slid inside. "This case has been my entire life for five years, and even a genius like Marley was desperate for a decent clue, but you'll probably have it solved before lunch. Bright young fellow you are."

The faint evidence of dawn could be seen backlighting the distant mountains beyond the city, like a thin red slash cut across the world. Breath came out in sickly gray clouds from the few people on the street. Scrooge suddenly remembered the smell of severed fingers charring beside a tray of blackened gingerbread cookies. Beautifully wrapped gifts pushed inside the gutted bodies of a family lying beneath their own Christmas tree. Nestled among the branches, between lights and decorations, their dripping tongues hung like ornaments.

A bus went roaring by, spraying the sidewalk with waves of filthy water. Bobby was saying something, but Scrooge couldn't make

11

out the words. They didn't seem to matter. On the corner, a figure in a grubby Santa suit stood atop a plastic milk crate ringing a bell and screaming, "The most wonderful tiiiiiiime of the yeeeeear!!!"

Behind Santa, Scrooge saw another person standing nearby: a young woman in dark jeans, high boots, and a black leather jacket adorned with tiny silver chains that sparkled as she bent to drop a dollar into the singing man's jar. An extreme amount of blood loss had given her complexion a distinctly corpse-like pallor. If anything, she somehow looked even more dead than when Scrooge saw her last: spread out on a slab in the city morgue almost exactly one year ago.

"No," Scrooge said through clenched teeth. "I don't believe it."

Nearly half the woman's head was missing, a gory crater of exposed bone and brain all that remained in its place. The hair clinging to the other half was matted and sticky with blood and ragged bits of flesh. Little crimson rivers, hot enough to steam in the chill morning air, ran down over her face. She smiled, raising one hand to wave, and with her still-intact eye, Marley Graves winked at her old partner.

"Even if you don't believe me," Bobby said, as Scrooge sat frozen behind the wheel, "I really do hope that you have a very Merry—"

"Stop." Scrooge reached to close the door. "If you finish that sentence, I'll have to tear off your arm and beat you to death with it."

In Emerald City and its surrounding environs, those seeking such entertainments could find boobs or booze, but rarely both at the same time.

Washington was, in fact, the only state in the entire country that banned the sale of alcohol in adult entertainment venues. Given that constraint, and the common practice of many club owners demanding a sizeable chunk of a dancer's tips to "rent" stage time, in lieu of funding the business primarily through the sale of overpriced drinks, the industry had long struggled in the Evergreen State.

Today, however, Tailfeathers was enjoying a comparatively brisk trade.

It was about 3 p.m. and the crowd had grown to a decent size. Nobody expected a packed house this early, but Belle hoped things would be going a little better by now. It was a holiday, after all. Everyone couldn't have familial obligations to keep them busy. Weren't there a few people looking to escape the cloying schmaltz and suffocating sentimentality of the season, even if just for the length of a lap dance or two?

Annabelle Hewitt, known to everyone as Belle, stood at the club's buffet table and filled a plastic cup with eggnog—nonalcoholic, of course. Her long blonde hair was pulled back in twin braids and, while her clothes and makeup were simple, Belle's fingernails were ornately painted neon blue with white tips and tiny glittering snowflake decals.

She was a tall woman with a fair complexion, thick in all the right places, but nicely toned thanks to good genes and many years spent dancing for a living. Though self-conscious about the lines that seemed to be inexorably deepening around her eyes and mouth, when Belle caught sight of herself passing in front of the club's many mirrors or slipped easily into a pair of faded jeans old enough to vote, even she had to admit she was holding up admirably for a working single mother inching further into middle age every day.

Belle turned away from the eggnog and looked over the club, which her dancers had decorated for the season with wreaths, fake snow, and many strands of multi-colored lights. All three stages were occupied by girls twirling and twerking, while patrons sat at low tables near the railing that circled each. Other guests congregated at the bar, where a lithesome redhead named Nikki mixed holiday mocktails. Reflexively, Belle began counting heads.

Yes, this Christmas Eve scheme of hers wasn't really doing so badly. And it was still early. Anything could happen.

In the years she'd owned Tailfeathers, Belle had tried many initiatives to attract more customers and ingratiate the club to the community, doing her best to relieve the stigma of the industry and prove that adult fun didn't necessarily have to be sleazy. Past attempts included hosting live music, staging bikini car washes to support local charities, topless talent shows with cash prizes, and offering free pole dancing classes.

Today, Belle's girls took turns occupying the stages for three songs apiece, dancing as best they could to the least-objectionable Christmas music the club's DJ could scrounge up. The others, meanwhile, except for Nikki at the bar, busied themselves accepting donations for the city-wide toy drive, doling out the proper rewards to the good boys (and a few good girls) who came to contribute. *Present a receipt with your donation and get one free private dance for every $30 spent!*

Even more popular was the gift wrapping service. Gorgeous gals wearing nothing but elf hats and smiles giggling and jiggling as they wrapped presents in festive paper and ribbons. Exhausted customers on their way home after a frantic morning of last-minute shopping got a show and much-appreciated service for the suggested tip of just ten dollars per item—plus whatever they decided the hefty helping of eye candy was worth on top of that.

Belle tasted the eggnog and wished desperately for a shot (or two) of whiskey. Although the governor had recently signed a law mandating the repeal of the state's longtime prohibition on serving alcohol in strip clubs, change was (so far) infuriatingly slow to come. Every preacher and politician opposed should be forced to drink a big cup of this pancake batter, she thought, bristling at the restriction—at *any* restriction.

She never was one to take orders well.

A rambunctious girl who spent her childhood ping-ponging back and forth between bitterly divorced parents, Belle learned early on how to read people and get attention when she wanted it, and how to disappear when she didn't. After high school, she muddled through a brief turbulent stint in the military, enlistment being the quickest guaranteed way to escape her hardscrabble hometown. But for Uncle Sam, too, she'd been fundamentally incapable of falling in line. Now, here again, people were trying to tell her what to do.

Belle had spent a great deal of time campaigning against the so-called "lewd conduct law" after relocating to Washington from

Las Vegas with her son, Tim. Having funded the move—a rushed midnight escape from her abusive partner, Tim's father—and the start of their new lives in the Pacific Northwest with money she'd earned dancing in Sin City, Belle was a true believer in the importance of the exotic entertainment industry and its potential, if properly regulated, to empower women.

Stripping was an occupation she'd entered reluctantly, but quickly discovered it to be profitable and even sometimes enjoyable. Plus, the nocturnal schedule allowed her to attend college courses during the day and care for Tim, which became all the more imperative after the boy was diagnosed with severe asthma. Although Washington's climate wasn't ideal for Tim's condition, Belle reasoned that the increasingly frequent beatings dished out to them both by the boy's father sure as hell hadn't been doing him any favors either.

Thinking of her son sent Belle toward her office in search of her phone. There was no school during the holiday break and although Tim was a good kid, who she trusted to stay home alone, he was still a teenage boy with lots of extra free time on his hands right now. She was due for another motherly check-in.

As Belle passed the stage, Desiree, a curvaceous black woman with long platinum dreads, stopped shimmying to *Santa Baby*, bent down, and motioned for her to come closer. "You have a visitor," she jerked a thumb at the door of Belle's office, which was closed.

Belle looked to the club's entrance. "Where the hell is Big Mack? Why am I paying for a bouncer if anybody can just walk in here and get into my office?"

Desiree winked and blew a kiss to the men gathered at the stage's rail, holding up one placating finger. "Dude brushed by Mack like it was nothing. Figured you'd want a heads up. Big white guy. Older, but still kind of cute. Everything about him screamed *cop* to me."

"Oh," Belle smiled. "I wasn't expecting to see him for a while."

"Is this going to be trouble?" Desiree was a new transplant to Seattle and fresh addition to the club's roster. She clearly hadn't decided yet how safe the place was and didn't recognize Scrooge. Big Mack did, though, and knew enough to get out of the man's way—especially at Christmastime.

"Maybe," Belle said, "but not the kind you mean."

She thanked Desiree and went into her office, closing the door behind her. It was a small dimly lit room, clean but cluttered, with thick black carpeting and several bubbling lava lamps placed in strategic locations. Humphrey Bogart and Ingrid Bergman stood cheek-to-cheek in a framed *Casablanca* poster above a couch seemingly made of more silver duct tape than brown leather. Beside the sad sofa was an antique heart-shaped glass table ringed by three extremely pink tufted velvet chairs, all of which Belle found at a flea market several years ago. Over one, a familiar beige coat had been tossed. Scrooge sat behind Belle's desk, pouring himself a hefty splash of bourbon from the bottle she kept in the bottom drawer.

"You got a warrant?" she asked, flipping the lock and striding over to him.

Scrooge drained the cup with a wince. "Please, no games today, Belle. I'm not in the mood."

She heard in his voice several hours of heavy drinking—several very productive hours, evidently, given that it showed at all despite the man's miraculous tolerance for alcohol. Belle stood between his knees, fists planted on her hips. "Whose playing? There are laws about this sort of thing. Now show me your warrant, Detective."

Scrooge reached for the bottle and Belle's hand went to his crotch, her grip tight enough to make him sit bolt upright, nearly dropping the whiskey.

"Guess I'll have to search you for it. What do we have here? A weapon perhaps? Pretty small caliber, I'd say. Probably nothing to worry about. But wait, what's this? It's growing bigger!"

Truthfully, not much was happening inside Scrooge's pants. Age and intoxication had come together in an unfortunate, but inevitable, sabotage. Unperturbed, Belle moved her hand to tousle the remnants of his hair instead. "I guess your meeting went as well as you expected?"

"What makes you say that?"

"It's pretty early and you're pretty drunk."

"So?" Scrooge poured the glass halfway full. "I'm drinking because it's the holidays and because I'm on vacation. Isn't this what people do when they're on vacation?"

Belle took the glass and sipped the smokey liquor. "What the hell are you talking about?"

Scrooge took back the drink and drained it before ranting his way through a brief, profanity-laden recap of the meeting at police headquarters.

"Fuck 'em, babe." Belle sat on the edge of her desk, legs draped across Scrooge's lap. "You tried your best. And you did your time wading through that mess already. If they want somebody else to take charge, let them."

"I don't know why I care." Scrooge glared into the empty glass. "People die every day, it's nothing special. Since the first humans climbed down from the trees, we've been hurting each other and killing each other and for what? It all ends in the grave eventually."

"Cheerful thought." Belle said. "I know you don't really mean that, but it's true there's nothing you can do except be gracious when they inevitably beg you to come back onto the case. And since you're here now," she leapt up and went to one of the scuffed filing cabinets slouching against the wall, "I have something for you."

From the topmost drawer, Belle took a small package covered with shiny decorative paper and tossed it to Scrooge. "I wrapped this one myself," she said, "but feel free to imagine that I did so in the buff, if you'd like."

"I told you how I feel about Christmas. And that includes presents."

"Yes, I've heard it all before: Christmas is bad, gifts are lame, nobody should be happy, blah, blah, blah. Good thing you're cute when you're grumpy, old man. But did it ever occur to you this particular present might be for somebody else, *Scrooge?*"

"Don't call me that."

"Sorry, just trying to lighten the mood. I know how stressful this time of year is for you and figured you wouldn't have time to do any shopping. So I picked something up and thought you could give it to Ellen when you see her."

At the mention of his daughter, Scrooge seemed to sink a little further into the chair. He cradled the gift in his large rough hands, staring into the gaudy wrapping as if looking for something.

"It's nothing fancy," Belle said to his silence. "I know that teenagers are hard to shop for, believe me. But I think she'll like this."

"Ellen's in Hawaii." Scrooge's voice was low and flat. "Her mother thought it would be good to get her out of Seattle this year. '*What with all that's going on,*' she said. And I didn't argue. The kid doesn't want to see me anyway. I was never Father of the Year material, but what can I do? She never answers my calls or texts. Too little, too late on my part, I guess. Fair enough."

"I'm sure it'll be fine if you just give her some space." Forcing a cheerier note into her voice, Belle said, "Why don't you come to my place tonight? Tim would love it. He asks all the time when you're coming over again. Go home first and change into something comfy. I'm making lasagna and we always watch *The Nightmare Before Christmas*. Then later, when Tim goes to bed, we can do some unwrapping of our own."

Scrooge stood up. "I'm going home. And I'm staying there."

"Are you sure?"

"Definitely."

"Why'd you say it like that?"

"Because I'm not interested in playing house with you and your sickly kid, Belle. Honestly, I never was. The last time was a mistake. And just because we fucked a few times doesn't mean you need to start picking out matching pajamas for the whole happy family."

"Please," Belle said, moving swiftly to open the door, "don't strain yourself doing me any favors. You don't want to come over tonight, that's fine. But you can go straight to Hell if you think I'm going to be your sexy little distraction whenever you see fit to drop by. And if you talk that way about my son again, I will kick your ass. Trust me, nobody is begging you to stick around, you depressing motherfucker. What did you even come here for if you're just going to be an asshole?"

"Another mistake," Scrooge said, pulling on his coat. "Seems like I'm on a roll."

"Well keep rolling, buddy, and maybe someday soon you'll hit the bottom." Just before she slammed the door in Scrooge's face, Belle said, "I'm way past the point in my life when I was dumb enough to find selfish dickheads attractive. If you're determined to be alone, I'm not going to stop you."

Scrooge turned and caught his reflection in the wall of mirrors behind the stage where Desiree was doing impressive things on the pole. Standing among the small crowd of gawking men, he saw Marley. The decorative lights glinted off the chains on her jacket as she raised a hand, but not to wave. This time, Marley pointed at her watch, the hands of which hung limp and useless. *No time.* The atrocity of Marley's face was not improved by the return of the smile she'd worn on the street earlier.

"Alone." Scrooge met Marley's stare, speaking too quietly to be heard above the blaring synth-heavy remix of *Winter Wonderland,* but knowing that she understood him perfectly, nonetheless. "Wouldn't that be nice?"

Scrooge lived in a small apartment in an aberrantly old and shabby building in Seattle's otherwise trendy Capitol Hill neighborhood. The unsightly artifact had so far escaped the area's rampant redevelopment, and all-but-complete campaign of gentrification, because of a complicated legal disagreement between the owner and city officials regarding its status as supposedly "historical."

The exterior façade was still white (more or less) when seen in the right light, although the cracks were growing more difficult to ignore with each passing year. Once, it had been considered a rather fancy hotel, but those days had long since gone the way of Model Ts and switchboard operators.

A hideously carpeted lobby, the original front desk and office spaces, which were now filled with rust-speckled laundry machines prone to leaks and a bank of mailboxes with regularly broken locks, sat below four loudly creaking floors holding six rooms each. The corner units, advertised as "luxury suites" in the lucrative days of yesteryear, were larger and included balconies and private bathrooms. Residents of the smaller apartments were forced to share communal facilities. Occupying the closest room on each floor was something of a mixed blessing, as it meant a shorter walk but more noise. Minus some dust, the building's walls were as thin as Egyptian parchment.

The combined racket of his neighbors' every word and move, plus the strained sounds of the building's ancient heating and plumbing systems, along with the nightly shrieking of a stray cat chorus which called the tiny lot behind the building home, was a cacophony to which Scrooge had never grown accustomed. In the years he had lived alone in a tiny unit on the decrepit building's top floor, he'd yet to sleep through the night without the aid of alcohol.

Now, a nearly empty bottle of whiskey sat on a TV tray beside his pistol. Scrooge's attention wandered between the items from where he sat, slumped in one of a pair of identical black leather recliners, which, aside from a boxy television perched on a peeling wooden cabinet, comprised the room's only furniture. He wore a sleeveless undershirt, exposing the tightly corded muscles of his pale arms and smudged shadows of old blue-green tattoos. He nodded, as if having arrived at some important conclusion after long and thorough debate, reached for the whiskey, and took a swallow.

Outside the window, icy wind went howling past. Though it was early yet, the night was already completely dark, with no stars or moon visible through the swirling mass of black clouds. Somewhere far below, the building's furnace came noisily to life and the room was filled with the clanking and rattling of its efforts. Among those sounds, the faint clinking of chains was difficult to distinguish—but not impossible. Scrooge drank again and cast his narrowed gaze onto the door.

"Don't even think about it," he growled.

The clinking grew louder.

"I will not allow this bullshit to continue." Scrooge drained the bottle and lobbed it at the door, but missed and it struck the wall instead. Even the smashing of glass could barely be heard over the awful din, which filled the small apartment with an almost physical presence.

"Go ahead, raise all the hell you want. It doesn't bother me."

Silence washed over the room like a tidal wave, sudden and complete. The TV came flickering to life, its screen a blazing portal of electronic snow. Overhead, the light dimmed, then went out completely. Scrooge scooped up the pistol and leaned forward, elbows on his knees.

"Fine. You always did have to get your way, didn't you? Let's go ahead and get this over with."

She entered without a flourish, as if it were the most natural thing in the world for a nearly headless woman to come strolling through a locked door on Christmas Eve. The chains on her leather jacket tinkled almost musically as Marley Graves surveyed the apartment with her single eye, and exposed when she turned the spectacle of her shattered skull and brain. She looked Scrooge over carefully before moving to the empty recliner.

"You don't sit in this chair naked, do you?"

"I wouldn't have thought ghosts cared about stuff like that."

"This one does." Marley shifted, as if trying to get comfortable. "I'd ask how you find women willing to spend the night here, but knowing your charming ass like I do, I think that's probably an issue that doesn't come up very often."

"You certainly sound like yourself," Scrooge said. "So I guess that means I'm either much drunker than I thought or there is something really strange happening here. Alright, I'll play along. What do you want, Marley?"

She looked around the room with an expression of disgust creeping across what remained of her face. "I'd honestly forgotten what a shithole this place is."

"Feel free to leave anytime."

"Soon enough, old man. I'm actually not allowed to stay long. And I can't tell you how I got here or where I've been, so don't bother asking. There are rules about this sort of thing and they are nonnegotiable. Suffice it to say that I'm here to help—in more ways than one."

"Lucky me." Scrooge laid the pistol on the tray and hefted himself from his chair. "If this is really going to happen, I need a beer. Be sure to get my attention again for the important part of the speech I sense coming up."

"Might want to lay off the sauce, my friend." Marley slowly rubbed her hands together. "You've got a looooong night ahead of you."

Scrooge collapsed back into the chair with two cold cans of Rainier. He passed one to Marley. "The only thing I have ahead of me," he said, cracking open the other, "is a hangover." His eyes strayed back to the pistol. "And maybe not even that."

Marley followed his gaze. "Did you know that death is not the end of pain? You and I were always so certain of the finality of death, but it turns out even the dead can suffer. Not from injury or illness or anything so tedious—we leave that crap to you *breathers*—but a lack of resolution pains us plenty. Unfinished business hurts, you understand? If a person dies without feeling fulfilled, if they have not been recognized for their achievements or held accountable for their actions, it's like a spiritual cancer that eats away at them for all eternity."

"You've been dead less than a year, Marley," Scrooge belched. "That hardly makes you an authority on eternity."

"Just shut up and listen, okay? I'm trying to explain some important cosmic shit here, if you don't mind." Marley opened her beer, slurped loudly, then raised a toast. "Cheers."

"Cheers," agreed Scrooge. They touched cans.

"Merry Christmas," Marley beamed.

"Fuck no," Scrooge said. "I will not drink to this bullshit holiday. You of all people should understand that."

"But that's exactly what I'm trying to tell you. I do understand... Or I did, at least." A new expression came over Marley's face, one that, if her features were more intact, might have read as sadness. "Christmas again already. Just one year ago, but it feels like so much longer. I had it, man. I had it all figured out. I even knew the bastard's name, I'm pretty sure."

Scrooge no longer cared if the situation was simply a product of intoxication or depression. He pushed aside the increasingly insistent notion that maybe he'd already pulled the trigger and blown his brains all over the wall of his shitty apartment. The vague suspicion this was some kind of bizarre hallucination concocted by his dying mind, like a strange twist on the light-at-the-end-of-the-tunnel thing, or floating above your own body.

"You found out who Humbug is?"

"I think so."

"Then tell me and I'll bag the son of a bitch before he kills another family tomorrow!"

"I can't," she whispered. "I can't remember anymore."

Marley tapped a finger against the soft meat of her brain. "That's how it works over there. Some things you recall vividly. And other things, even really important things, the kinds of things you tell yourself you couldn't possibly forget in a million years, they vanish. Poof! Like a dream."

"Isn't that convenient?" Scrooge gulped down most of his beer. "Still, I can think of more than a few things I wouldn't mind forgetting."

"I don't think *forgetting* is in the immediate future for you." Marley put her drink on the floor and made a show of checking her broken wristwatch. "In fact, quite the opposite. For now you'd best get ready to receive company. You already know where this is going, right? It's Christmas Eve and you, my grumpy old friend, are in dire need of some perspective. After all, it was good enough for Mickey and the Muppets and Bill Murray. You are about to get a helpful consultation from a rather ghostly source. Three sources, technically."

"What are you talking about?"

"Think hard, *Scrooge*."

"Don't call me that."

"I always thought it was a pretty fitting nickname—especially for tonight."

Scrooge's eyes widened. "Marley, no. I was willing to humor you, but this? No way."

"Yes way. Scrooge, listen closely. You will be visited—"

"Don't say it."

"Sorry, pal." Marley raised her hands, wiggled her fingers, and in a perfect imitation of an old-timey TV horror host ominously intoned, "You will be visited by Three Spirits!"

"Jesus fucking Christ."

"Afraid not. Men like you are assigned ministers of a very different sort. Ones who hail from other regions and who bring with them other messages. But as unpleasant as they are—and, oh boy, are they unpleasant!—you must heed the lessons of these spirits. It's the only way for you to repair your life, catch the killer, and save yourself. And me, too."

She stood, laid a hand on the TV, and the screen blinked instantly into darkness. "It hurts, Scrooge. It hurts like you could never understand to die with so much left undone. All my life I cared only for the job. I thought only of the hunt, the chase. Of being the smartest person in the room. I neglected so much about the experience of being alive. How all that emptiness eats at me now!"

Marley fixed Scrooge with a mad glare and pointed at him with one trembling finger.

"I would spare you that agony, but you have to do the work. Tonight's your chance—your *only* chance. I had to call in some serious favors and search very dark places to find the spirits you'll meet tonight. You see, in their own twisted way, they also know what it's like to suffer the pain of unfinished business. It wasn't pleasant, asking for their help. And what comes next won't be pleasant for you. But I went through it because I'm still rooting for you, old man. You believed in me back when nobody else on the force did. Because you were the only one willing to be my partner and always had my back. Because you were my friend."

She walked to the door, boots crunching on the shards of whiskey bottle scattered on the dingy carpet.

"And I think you'll go through it because deep down you aren't ready to punch your own ticket just yet. There's a killer on the loose and lives are at stake—souls, too. I know you well enough to be sure you're no quitter. Besides, it's Christmas. A season of miracles. The one time of year when salvation is not impossible. Not even for the likes of you."

Scrooge weighed the pistol in one hand. "Marley," he said, "it's been fun. Really, thanks for dropping by. But if you actually knew me at all you'd realize what a waste of time this little performance was."

He brought the barrel of the gun up beneath his chin, saying, "Fuck Christmas and fuck all that corny Dickens crap," then pulled the trigger.

THE BUTCHER'S LAMENT
(CHRISTMAS PAST)

The **Cleveland Torso Murderer**, also known as the **Mad Butcher of Kingsbury Run**, was an unidentified <u>serial killer</u> who was active in <u>Cleveland</u>, <u>Ohio</u>, United States, in the 1930s. The killings were characterized by the <u>dismemberment</u> of thirteen known victims and the disposal of their remains in the impoverished neighborhood of <u>Kingsbury Run</u>. Most victims came from an area east of Kingsbury Run called "The Roaring Third" or "Hobo Jungle," known for its bars, <u>gambling</u> dens, <u>brothels</u>, and <u>vagrants</u>. Despite an investigation of the murders, which at one time was led by famed lawman <u>Eliot Ness</u>, the murderer was never apprehended.

– Wikipedia

Scrooge woke up lying face down on the floor, fireworks of pain exploding behind his eyes. He forced himself onto his hands and knees, nearly toppled over, but righted himself. Noticing the pistol nearby on the carpet, he brought a hand to his face and tentatively probed. He was, it seemed, unharmed.

A misfire, he thought? *A dream, more likely. Some kind of booze- and stress-fueled nightmare.*

Or maybe he'd succeeded in his suicide attempt and was now a ghost? Scrooge struggled to his feet, thinking he was in too much pain to be dead. Every move made his skull rattle. His bones felt as if they'd grown thorns. He was glad for the dark, the overhead light and TV being off, as even the concept of brightness made him wince.

How long was I out?

Scrooge wore no watch and the window remained an unhelpful black void. Also, his cellphone was missing from his pocket, so Scrooge had no idea what time it was. But that particular mystery was not terribly troubling. This was far from the first time he'd woken up on the floor after a bender. The ache in his head, too, was hardly a new experience. Scrooge knew exactly what to do next. After the surreal ordeal of being haunted (if that was indeed what just happened) this was familiar territory again. And the pain, terrible as it was, was also comfortingly real in its own way. In his suffering and anger, Scrooge felt like himself again.

He hobbled into the kitchenette, filled a glass from the faucet and swallowed three pills from the Costco-sized bottle of aspirin on the counter. Putting the empty cup into the sink, Scrooge next moved to retrieve the pistol before he was stopped short by a sudden flurry of snapping fingers. Dozens of fingers, it seemed, snapping together as if in applause. He looked around for the source of the sound and froze when a strange shape shuffled out of the room's far corner.

The perfect amalgamation of man and maggot. A bloodlessly pale head, round, bald, and far too large for the long skinny neck on which it rode. Dominating the face were two gaping wounds in place of eyes, both weeping tears of vile smelly pus. Around the creature's mouth, inside of which was a forest of yellowed needle-like teeth, sprouted a ring of filth-smeared fingers growing out of its face like tentacles, all wiggling and snapping excitedly.

"What says you, Lawman?" The voice was calm and weirdly gentle. Singularly soft, as if instead of speaking to him from across the room, the creature was whispering directly into Scrooge's ear. "Would you guzzle liquor and cower alone in the dark? Or might you be enticed to brave a holiday jaunt with a new friend on this stark and bitter Christmas Eve?"

A thin figure, tall but badly hunched. Standing straight, his head would easily graze the ceiling. As it was, he seemed bent nearly in half, long torso angled sharply forward and snaking through the air ahead of his legs. The hairless white skin of his body was stretched over prominent bones, which jutted out sharply from his back and shoulders. A line of four spindly arms dangled from both his sides, each of the hands' tiny fingers snapping continuously in time with those around his mouth.

"I don't have any friends," Scrooge said, unable to take his eyes off the terrible intruder. "And I don't celebrate Christmas."

The creature wore rough trousers, chunky boots, and a stained apron as might be seen on a butcher, heavily smeared with gore. He moved closer, causing the bladed instruments which hung from his belt to clatter together like gruesome windchimes.

"So I've been told, how unfortunate. There are only so many moments in life truly worth celebrating. Quite a shame, I'd say, especially for a man like you, one with so little time remaining, to reject even a single one while he still has some choice in the matter."

Scrooge reached for the pistol and was immediately made confident by the weight and feel of it in his hand, like enjoying the unconditional support of an old friend. "You must be the first of the guests Marley told me to expect. I was prepared for a ghost or maybe the robed specter of Death, all that melodramatic English Lit stuff. But what the hell are you supposed to be?"

The creature's head weaved in the air before Scrooge, fingers around its mouth spreading open to show a smile which revealed all of its many teeth. "I have been called the Mad Butcher of Kingsbury Run and the Cleveland Torso Murderer. To some, I was the Boogeyman. I ruled as King of the Beasts in the fearsome Hobo Jungle and left my bloody mark on the Untouchable One himself. Tonight, however, I am proud to simply be the Ghost of Christmas Past."

Scrooge said, "Sounds like the ancient past to me."

The Butcher chuckled. It was a terrible sound, wet and bubbly, like somebody choking on their own blood. "More like *your* past, Lawman."

"My past is my business." Scrooge leveled the gun at his unwelcome guest. "Now get to the point, freakshow. Why are you here?"

"Your welfare."

"Don't fuck with me, you creepy son of a bitch."

"Your reclamation, then. Take heed, Lawman!" The Butcher spread his eight skeletal arms and forced Scrooge to lock eyes with his septic gaze. "Redemption and vindication lie within."

The spirit was upon Scrooge in an instant, far too quickly to allow for a response or reaction. Hands like shackles closed around the detective's wrists, pried the pistol from his grasp, and forced him to the floor.

When he tried to scream, Scrooge found another of the hideous ghost's many hands clamped tightly across his mouth. Helpless, he could only watch as the Butcher drew from his belt an imposingly long chef's knife. The blade effortlessly cut away Scrooge's thin undershirt, the edge painfully cold where it pressed into the soft flesh of his belly.

"Not so long ago, in Rome," the Butcher's voice was seductive and low, "mystics read entrails as a way of communing with the gods. Not merely to foresee the future, you understand. No, they hoped to ascertain how their communities might behave so as to achieve a state of harmony between the human and divine."

Scrooge felt himself being slit open.

"Those same Romans capped each December with a raucous, drunken banquet honoring the god Saturn, to whom they offered dead and dying warriors in adoring supplication. Such wonderful gifts—squirming red, wet Christmas presents wrapped in flesh—to be ripped open and enjoyed by the god of time, wealth, and liberation. Mortals concern themselves with little else, would you not agree, beyond time, wealth, and liberation? Long and bloody is the legacy of this season, Lawman. Is it so odd, then, for the killer you seek to have chosen it as the time of their own sacrificial rites?"

A hot flood of bile, blood, and intestines spilled across Scrooge's lap. He smelled the rancid stench of his own bowels as the Butcher's thin fingers pried open the gash and explored, probing and digging, clawing their way deeper inside of him.

"The meat retains what the mind would eliminate."

Pain like an all-consuming blaze exploded outward from the core of his guts to incinerate every inch of Scrooge's conscience. He squeezed his eyes shut and heard the roaring of his own blood in his ears, a racing pulse behind which, faintly, he detected new voices. Furious voices that were ominously familiar.

A woman shouted. A man responded. Glass was shattered. And in that moment he understood the horrific destination toward which they were bound.

Please no, Scrooge's mind begged. *Not that.*

Anything but them.

The agony vanished in a blink and Scrooge found himself standing in a different shabby room. It was instantly familiar to him, though: the rough fabric of the green carpet, ancient sofa and matching loveseat, streaky beige paint on the walls. In one corner was an artificial Christmas tree of a strikingly vintage silver color, adorned with red ornaments in the shapes of stars, candy canes, and snowmen. Beneath it were several small and oddly shaped packages wrapped in old newspaper.

Again, Scrooge found he was unharmed with no sign of his mutilation by the ghost now visible on the skin beneath his shirt, which was also intact. He walked slowly around the room, registering a thousand simultaneous thoughts, smells, memories, and feelings long forgotten. The experience was dizzying and returned the faintest trace of his hangover, a queasiness in his stomach and slight pounding at his temples.

He ran his fingers over the framed photographs on the wall, staring intently at the child in each: a little boy with a fixed expression of grim determination and startlingly light blue eyes. Somewhere in the next room, the unseen woman screamed again, more glass was broken. Giggling, the Butcher came sliding out from behind the metallic tree.

"This place," he asked, "…it is familiar to you?"

"Yeah," Scrooge said. "I grew up in this house."

The deep male voice bellowed and thunderous footsteps seemed to shake the entire world. Scrooge instinctively retreated one step, then another, pressing his back to the wall.

"And are they, too, familiar, Lawman?" The Butcher inclined his head toward the doorway, the altercation transpiring in the next room.

"Yes," Scrooge whispered.

"Strange to have forgotten them for so many years."

"I did my best. It got easier, eventually. After they died."

The Butcher nodded. "These are but shadows of the things that have been. They have no awareness of us and we cannot affect them."

The woman was screaming again.

"She appears to be upset." The Butcher fixed Scrooge with the unblinking wounds of his eyes. "She's raving."

"She was always raving. My mother was a lunatic and my father was a tyrant. The perfect pairing for misery and abuse all around. Give it a minute, I promise the old man will take his turn at bat."

A sound like hammers striking a thick side of beef was followed by silence. Then came the pained noise of someone struggling to breathe. The man's voice was a low rumble, so much like a growl.

"My parents," Scrooge said. "By all rights one should have killed the other a million times over. But the only thing they hated more than each other was the idea of being alone."

The Butcher raised a hand and pointed to the far corner of the room. "But they were not alone."

Scrooge said he knew, voice catching in his throat.

They watched as a child crept silently down the narrow staircase. His head was lowered, shoulders slumped, one side of his pale face marred by a violet bruise. And although he'd since grown by several years, he was obviously the little boy from the photographs. A child Scrooge knew very, very well.

The Butcher said, "He also appears upset."

"He usually was."

"Do you recall this particular disagreement?"

"There were so many." Scrooge listened as his mother wailed in the next room and further off, in the kitchen, his father noisily searched cupboards for a bottle that was not yet empty. Tears escaped from the crouching boy's tightly closed eyelids. Scrooge's hands ached as his fingernails bit into his palms. "What the hell are we doing here? How is this supposed to help me catch Humbug?"

"I don't know why you care." The fingers on the Butcher's face drummed thoughtfully against his mouth. "Since the first humans climbed down from the trees, we've been hurting each other and killing each other."

"That doesn't mean you don't try," Scrooge said. "It doesn't mean we can't make things better sometimes."

"Tell me about some better times." The Butcher reached out to absently toy with an ornament dangling from the tree, twisting the crimson ball this way and that, watching it catch and reflect the light. "Was there no one with whom you spent even a single enjoyable holiday?"

"Nobody," Scrooge said. "The other kids made fun of me for being poor and having a couple of psychos for parents. None of the adults cared about my bruises and broken bones, it was a very different time back then. I had to do odd jobs so we could afford to keep the heat on all winter. And every year at Christmas my parents seemed to get more violent while the rest of the world went around smiling ear to ear and singing their stupid hearts out. I've always hated this fucking holiday."

The Butcher flashed his teeth. "Are you certain?"

They walked together, Scrooge and the Butcher, through a neighborhood. Despite the cold, the heavy snow blanketing the world around them, regardless of his insufficient attire, Scrooge felt no chill.

He knew the place well enough that he could have moved through it blindfolded, his feet found their way without a thought. It was his hometown, after all. Just another bland tract of American suburbia, perhaps, slightly run down and maybe a little more neglected than most, it was true. But the place was his hometown nonetheless. And people can never truly forget where they came from.

"My parents were something I survived," Scrooge said. "Like war or a terrible accident. I got away as soon as I could and never looked back."

Around them, holiday decorations glowed in the snowy darkness like beacons. The soft light coming from behind the closed blinds and window shades of the surrounding houses made the night seem that much darker. The strange pair's passage through the snow was silent and left no tracks.

"They died years ago, one right after the other. I didn't even go to the funerals. I used to feel bad about that." Scrooge stopped and looked around, as if confused as to where he was, how exactly he'd arrived there. "As I got older, I decided it didn't matter."

He searched his pockets. "I mean, who really cares, right? Plenty of people live perfectly happy lives never knowing their parents. Hell, I'd sometimes rather have not known my parents. It's nothing to cry about."

"What is the matter?" asked the Butcher.

"Nothing. It's nothing. I lost my phone back in my apartment and was thinking maybe my daughter would try to call tonight. I don't want her to think I was ignoring her if she did. That's all."

"And how, I wonder, did you intend to answer such a call with a bullet in your brain?" The Butcher's many fingers began snapping excitedly. "Are you absolutely certain there was nothing enjoyable about the holidays for you as a child?"

"Yes! For Christ's sake, I already told you."

"Then tell me what, if anything, do you recall about this place?" The Butcher gestured with all his arms toward the modest ranch-style house they now stood before.

The night fell away before Scrooge could answer. He found himself transported to a cozy room full of shelves overstuffed with books, warmly lit by several lamps, the floor covered by an ornate rug. It gave the immediate impression of being a place in which one could easily enjoy many peaceful hours. A record spun smoothly on the old turntable atop a cabinet in the corner, playing one of Johnny Cash's Christmas albums, the only concession to the holiday evident in the study.

Scrooge's younger self, at least a year or two older now, hair slightly longer and the bruise gone from his face, sat at a small table looking fixedly down at a game of chess. Across from him was an old man, brown eyes gleaming keenly behind thin silver glasses. He wore a tweed fedora and thick plaid shirt, the sleeves rolled up on his skinny arms to the elbows. His slightly crooked teeth clenched the stem of an unlit pipe. The record came to an end, the tonearm raised up and slid away, and the old man got stiffly out his chair to flip it.

The Butcher reclined on the sofa, gently sawing the air with a long serrated blade. "Tell me, Lawman, do you recognize him?"

Scrooge's face erupted in a smile. "Damn right, I do. That's old Fred Willkie. He was a retired cop who lived a few houses down from us. Used to pay me to do chores for him. The guy loved chess, must have tried to teach it to me a hundred times. But I never could figure out that stupid game."

The blade glinted as the Butcher gestured at the books surrounding them. "He also taught you something else, I believe."

Scrooge nodded and seemed about to speak.

"Well?" asked Fred, lowering the needle. "Can you see it yet?"

At the table, young Scrooge shook his head.

"Try a fresh angle. Go over to my seat and look again."

As the boy swapped seats, the old man struggled with shaking hands to light his pipe. "You have to be able to see it from the other guy's perspective, kid. That's the only way to know what he's thinking. What he'll do next. And once you know that, you'll beat him every time."

The boy sat back in the chair and knuckled his eyes. "But it's hard!"

"Of course it's hard." Fred eased himself into the empty seat. "If it were easy it wouldn't matter and anybody could do it. Look again. Take your time."

Scrooge laughed. "The old man looks like a harmless librarian, doesn't he? But I found out later he was a damn good cop. All the guys who worked with him said he was brilliant. They said he could get the wiliest bad guys to break down and give it up just by asking the right questions."

The Butcher shrugged his many shoulders. "Yet another criminologist geek. All he knows are *microfibers* and *behavior analysis.*

No way he had what it takes to handle a hostile suspect." He sliced the air with his blade. "No guts."

"This man was better than that." Scrooge said. "He never had to resort to beating a confession out of anybody."

"A small matter," said the Butcher, "...to outwit a few petty thieves and desperate junkies."

"Small?" echoed Scrooge.

"Is it not? A man reads a few books, takes notes, and speaks more quietly and patiently than most so as to appear more adept than he really is. How would he fare, I wonder, against the likes of a true predator?"

"There's more to the job than taking notes and speaking softly," said Scrooge, heated by the remark and speaking decidedly *less* softly than his childhood mentor might. "And I'll have you know that if Fred were still on the force, we'd have bagged Humbug years ago. He would have it all figured out so fast it'd make your ugly head spin. That's how the great ones work: calmly and quietly. They don't need to bluster or bully anybody because they're real detectives. That's how Fred worked. That's how Marley worked, too, and she was a genius."

Scrooge struck his palm with a fist. "Bobby works like that. In the year we've been partnered, I've seen it. The kid is always watching and listening to everything all the time, you can tell. Best move the chief could have made, picking Bobby to head up the Humbug case."

Scrooge felt the ghost's examining look and became quiet.

"What is the matter now?" asked the Butcher.

"Nothing. Never mind."

"Your anguish is intoxicating, Lawman. I think it's more than nothing."

"No," Scrooge said, his attention focused on some vague and indistinct place far away. "I shouldn't have been so rough on the kid this morning, that's all. It doesn't matter. He doesn't need my approval."

"Oh no?" The Butcher laughed, the same wet nightmarish sound.

At the table, Fred picked up the battered paperback lying beside the gameboard. "While you're thinking it over," he said to the boy, "tell me what you thought of *Murder on the Orient Express*."

"I hated that book," Scrooge said.

"I hated that book," the boy said. "They can't all have done it. That's cheating."

"*Cheating*?" Fred gasped. "My dear boy, that is Agatha Christie herself, the undisputed Queen of Crime, who you are disparaging. And this book is a revered classic of the genre."

"But it's not fair," the boy insisted.

"What's fair got to do with anything?"

In the corner, Scrooge agreed. "Goddamn right."

The old man got up and went to the nearest bookshelf, running one gnarled finger over the spines and squinting at their titles.

Young Scrooge sighed. "Can we please play a different game?"

"I have something better." Fred returned and laid a new book on the table. "Merry Christmas, kid. This one, I think you'll enjoy. Allow me introduce you to Mr. Nero Wolfe."

Scrooge watched his younger self read the first pages of Rex Stout's *Fer-de-Lance*, noting how Fred watched the boy as well. Both older men smiled.

"We read a lot of books together," Scrooge said. "It was fun, assembling the pieces of a mystery. Fred showed me how to make sense of the world and understand why things happened the way they did. I first decided I wanted to be a detective in this room."

The Butcher rose from the sofa. "There was, I believe, another important Christmas here."

Scrooge's face blanched. "Please, no. Not that year. Why are you doing this to me?"

"I told you already these are the shadows of things that have been. They are what they are. Do not blame me."

The room changed around them, aging and growing shabby. The old man became older, his illness more apparent. The boy vanished, and Scrooge watched his friend limping and shuffling weakly among his books and records, attention roaming constantly but never settling on anything in particular. He would select a title from the shelf, then put it down again moments later, unopened. On the table, the chess set became covered in a layer of dust. Every so often, Fred would wander to the telephone on a small table in the corner and dial. Although it went unanswered every time, without fail, he'd soon pause his aimless wanderings and make another attempt.

"Damn it," Scrooge growled, "I don't want to watch this."

"It's almost over," the Butcher told him. "Do you know who the old man was so intent upon reaching? I'm given to understand that most people experience a desire to speak to loved ones at Christmastime."

Fred's face went slack as he leaned heavily against a bookcase. One hand scrambled to his chest. From his straining throat, a weak keening sound escaped.

"Fuck you, I was working," Scrooge said. "I was busy."

"Yes," the Butcher nodded. "Busy being a detective, like this man inspired you to become. Although you turned out to be of a very different sort, isn't that so? What do you think he would have said if you'd bothered to answer the phone? And please remind me, how many days was it that he lay in this room before being discovered? Do you even remember? Five? Six?"

"I don't know."

"More than a week?"

"Fuck you."

"Then again," said the Butcher, "people die every day. Nothing special, right? It all ends in the grave eventually."

Fred collapsed into a shuddering whimpering heap on the dusty carpet. The acrid stink of piss filled the room.

Into Scrooge's ear, the Butcher whispered, "What do you know of the grave, Lawman? I stole many lives before shuffling off the coil myself and recall both experiences perfectly. Death is my native domain. Do you want to know how it feels? What your friend felt as he expired alone in this sad little room? Shall I tell you what waits on the other side of that thin veil? First comes a long and lonely walk in the dark. You will be alone in the end, Lawman, rest assured of that. And it's cold out there in the blackness. So very, very cold."

"FUCK YOU!"

Scrooge turned on the spirit, furious. But instead of the Butcher's malicious grin or Fred's bookshelves, he found himself looking over his own apartment, seemingly just as he'd left it. Scrooge saw himself seated just as before, in one of the twin recliners. Once again, a wobbly TV tray was in front of him and on it rested a bottle of whiskey and his pistol. This time, however, he was not alone.

"Do you promise you never sit here naked?" Marley reclined in the opposite chair, intact and very much alive. She watched the seated Scrooge as he took a deep swallow from the bottle. "Might want to lay off the sauce, my friend. We've got a long night ahead of us. And tomorrow promises to be a real bitch, too."

Not for you, Scrooge thought. He'd placed himself now, knew exactly where he was—and when. It was one year ago on Christmas Eve. Last Christmas Eve. It was Marley's last, and the final day of her life, not that either of them could have known it at the time of this conversation. Scrooge watched himself pull his phone from his pocket and silence the ringer.

"Ellen again?" asked Marley.

Scrooge grunted and reached for the bottle.

"Mark my words, old man. Someday soon you are going to wish that girl would deign to so much as text you now and then, let alone call."

"I guess you'd know," Scrooge said. "Just to be clear, exactly how many kids have you raised?"

"I may not be a parent. But which of us do you think knows more about the experience of being a daughter?"

"Why don't you focus that big brain of yours on the task at hand? Sometime in the next twenty-four hours we're going to get a call that sends us to the scene of yet another massacre committed by the same goddamn maniac we've been chasing for nearly half a decade. And we are no closer to nailing him tonight than on day fucking one. You're supposed to be brilliant, right? Well, how about it, genius? What's the plan?"

Marley stood and began to pace. Scrooge watched himself pointedly ignore his buzzing phone, the screen lighting up to display an image of Ellen holding a giant ice cream cone, and felt his face flush with shame and rage.

"There has to be something that links the families." Marley was whispering, talking mainly to herself. "A common factor. A connection."

"We've been through all that," the seated Scrooge groaned. "There's nothing."

"Nothing that we caught, but there has to be something. They're too much alike for there not to be."

Scrooge watched himself nip the bottle and sigh heavily before saying, "You got that part right. I mean honestly, these fucking people. Pampered, privileged, wealthy clones of each other. The same exact model number: *Suburban American Family 101*. It's like Humbug's picking them out of a catalogue or something. But just because they all look the same that doesn't mean they are. That type of thinking is called *profiling*, Marley, and it's very out of vogue in this business nowadays. Incredibly un-PC of you. Get the picture?"

Marley froze mid-step. Her eyes sparkled.

47

"What?" Scrooge drained the whiskey. "You okay?"

"Picture," Marley whispered. "Like in a catalogue."

Scrooge watched from the corner of the room as he hefted himself clumsily from the chair and lumbered into the kitchenette for a can of beer, belching loudly as he asked, "What the hell are you talking about, Marley?"

She grabbed her bulky leather jacket from a hook by the door and pulled it on, the tiny chains jingling as she said, "I'm not exactly sure. Might be nothing. But I need to look over some files down at HQ. You want to come with?"

Scrooge collapsed back into his chair, cracking open a can of Rainier. "Thanks, but I've looked enough. Our only hope now is that Humbug makes a mistake with the next family and leaves behind something we can use to nail him."

"You're probably right," Marley smiled and rubbed her hands together. "But I've got one hell of a hunch, Scrooge."

"Don't call me that."

"Sorry. It's just that if I'm right, which is a long shot, but if I am..."

"Anything you'd like to share with the class?" Just then, Scrooge's phone buzzed again, the glowing screen filled with the image of Ellen and her ice cream.

Marley looked from the grinning girl to her partner. "Talk to your fucking kid, asshole. I'll call if this turns out to be something."

"Take my car," Scrooge said. "The roads are dangerous tonight."

"You still don't get me at all, do you, old man? Marley swung open the door, helmet under one arm. "That's my favorite part."

As she left, the Butcher entered, sliding through the door as it closed behind Marley, who'd be dead a few hours later. Crushed beneath the speeding wheels of a truck after leaving police headquarters, intent on going...where? Nobody knew. Surveillance footage inside the building showed her pawing through the Humbug files, clearly looking for something. She examined a lot of photographs that night but didn't leave a note and didn't call her partner. Whatever she found, if she found anything, Marley Graves evidently decided to keep it to herself. And Scrooge was left to examine the next day's massacre on his own.

"Shall we tarry a moment and see if you made a phone call?" The Butcher leered at Scrooge. "Or might you remember that part unassisted?"

Scrooge wiped his face clean of tears with both palms and watched himself sit and drink alone in his shabby apartment.

"It's my fault," he whispered. "I let everyone down."

"Not me, Lawman." The Butcher stalked nearer, putrid tears of hideous joy glistening on his face. "Rest assured, you've proven just as deliciously tortured as I was promised."

Scrooge rushed the spirit, all pounding fists and gnashing teeth. The ghost was shockingly solid to the touch as he struck blow after blow, but Scrooge could still hear Fred's weakening gasps; the buzzing of his unanswered phone; booming of the door closing behind Marley and echo of her saying *talk to your fucking kid, asshole*; the awful wet sound of the Butcher's laugh, clearly delighted by his desperation.

With each punch, Scrooge saw a different face beneath his fists. Another suspect he'd roughed up and beaten. Another confession he'd earned by spilling blood. Oh yes, there had been plenty of confessions, but desperate human beings will admit to anything if you hurt them badly enough. And Scrooge was very adept at causing pain. A true professional.

Nobody is better in the room than you, every cop in the city knows that.

His fist collided painfully with frosty concrete and Scrooge wailed, feeling the winter wind cut across his exposed flesh. He had the insane thought he was battering his own gravestone, fighting the inevitability of eternity. It was dark and cold and he was truly alone.

Dead, Scrooge thought, *I'm already dead. The gun worked and I'm dead and this is going to last forever—nothing but icy blackness and regret.*

The agony in his hands forced him to focus. Looking up, confused and disoriented, Scrooge found himself on the sidewalk outside his apartment building. It was nighttime and snowing, the flakes gathering into little drifts and mounds. Scrooge shivered, but gratefully, knowing the pain meant he was still alive.

Stumbling toward his building, already trying to convince himself the events of the night so far had been nothing more than side effects of stress and alcohol—perhaps even alcohol poisoning, Scrooge thought; couldn't enough booze induce such hallucinations?—the wounded detective was taken aback to find the front door wide open.

He lurched into the lobby, which was dark and empty. *Maybe there'd been a power outage?* As his eyes adjusted, Scrooge saw the fog of his breath, thick and clear. Somehow, it was even colder in the building than it was outside. *What the hell was going on?*

Something crunched beneath his feet. Scrooge looked down to see he was walking on scattered sheets of paper. Old newspaper, it seemed, the pages yellowed and brittle. He shambled clumsily through the litter as a swirling breeze stirred the paper around his ankles, the sound very much like autumn leaves.

From the darkness came the noise of somebody moving forward, as if to meet him. A bulky figure, the shape of it indistinct but weighty, tangible—like a darker patch of shadow broken free of the night.

The voice, when they finally spoke, was masculine. Completely devoid of inflection or emotion, it held all the personality of a scalpel. The words found Scrooge's ears through a storm of static, as if the person were speaking through a bad landline phone connection. Little pops and scratches punctuated the affectless introduction.

"This is the Zodiac speaking..."

And the crinkling, crunching steps grew louder as he arrived.

"Peek-a-boo, You Are Doomed." (Christmas Present)

The Zodiac Killer is the pseudonym of an unidentified serial killer who operated in Northern California in the late 1960s. The case has been described as the most famous unsolved murder case in American history and has become both a fixture of popular culture and a focus for efforts by amateur detectives. The Zodiac murdered five known victims in the San Francisco Bay Area between December 1968 and October 1969, operating in rural, urban, and suburban settings... The Zodiac coined his name in a series of taunting messages that he mailed to regional newspapers, in which he threatened killing sprees and bombings if they were not printed. Some of the letters included cryptograms, or ciphers, in which the killer claimed that he was collecting his victims as slaves for the afterlife... Of the four ciphers he produced, two remain unsolved.

– Wikipedia

Amidst the ankle-deep sea of torn tabloids and crumpled newspaper pages in which he stood, Scrooge saw the smiling faces of murder victims and missing persons staring back at him. Bold headlines screamed of devastating fires, explosions, shooting sprees. Crumpled photographs captured scenes of the most perverse and violent pornography imaginable.

Seeming to rise up from the slew of victims and innumerable acts of savagery, Scrooge beheld a hulking figure made, apparently, of paper-mâché. Stories of murder and mayhem, rape and mutilation, had been shredded, reshaped, and plastered together into the form of a hunched man who moved steadily closer in a slow lumbering gait.

The letters and enigmatic symbols on Zodiac's stiff skin were a legion of fonts and sizes, and all of them seemed to glow as if written in streaks of smoldering fire. There was no mouth, but inside the twin hollows carved into the spirit's otherwise unsettlingly smooth and featureless face in place of eyes, tiny flames blazed. And as relieved as he was to find this specter at least possessed eyes of some sort, unlike his predecessor, Scrooge was nevertheless loathe to meet them. There seemed to be tortured figures writhing in those fires.

"I hope you are having lots of fun."

Again, the staticky voice seemed to whisper to Scrooge from someplace inside his own head.

"Present. Consider if you will, Detective, the word itself. It means to make a gift of something or bring it to someone's attention. To become manifest. Yet, it also means something currently existing or

in progress. To be at hand or in view. Most obviously, the word simply means Now. The present time."

The characters emblazed across Zodiac glowed more brightly as he spoke, tiny wisps of smoke curled up from his parchment flesh, and Scrooge detected the faint smell of burning.

"The hour is late, but now is the time. All the time there is, in fact. All the time you will ever have. We are here, manifested together in defiance of reason and logic, for one special moment. Crucial happenings are in progress, Detective. I am, in every sense, the Ghost of Christmas Present. And you are welcome."

Scrooge folded his arms and considered the spirit. "Pretty big talk for a pinata made of trash. This ain't my first ghostly rodeo, buddy. I'm not afraid. You lead and I'll follow. Just tell me something first, okay? Are you actually going to help me catch Humbug or not?"

With a sweep of his hand, Zodiac sent the pages on the floor up into the air and flying wildly about in a blinding, deafening maelstrom that filled the room.

"Man is the most dangerous animal of all. You speak of rodeos, Detective, somehow failing to see the reality of your situation. This search is a safari, not a rodeo. A wise man once said the world is made of only two classes: hunters and the hunted. To understand one you must first know the other."

Pages battered Scrooge with relentless ferocity. His skin was cut open in dozens of places, each tiny slice a new pain eclipsing the last. In a desperate attempt to protect his eyes, Scrooge cupped his hands over them and sank to the floor, curling into himself, hoping to become the smallest target possible. Still, he felt himself assaulted by the horrendous headlines and graphic photos. So much violence! So pervasive was the pain those pages held that Scrooge despaired. How could any society claiming itself to be a civilization withstand such wickedness?

Zodiac was humming a holiday song Scrooge couldn't name. It was familiar, almost annoyingly so, but he could not recall the title or who performed it. He had just enough time to enjoy a quick flash of memory—his daughter as a little girl tearing open a present on Christmas morning, both of them sitting on the floor beside the tree with the smell of fresh coffee brewing in the kitchen and the sound of his wife singing that same song, the words maddeningly unclear in his mind—before darkness overcame him. Blackness punctuated only by the scratchy static-filled humming of a gleeful murderer became his universe.

Last Christmas.

Feeling himself bleed from countless small wounds, the song's lyrics crystalized in Scrooge's mind. A tune so ubiquitous he hadn't realized he knew the words. A story so universal he'd stopped hearing it. A moral everybody knew so well they'd ceased to consider it.

Broken hearts and desperate hopes.

Agony and ecstasy—both equally inevitable.

Better days, maybe next year.

Last Christmas...

The house in which Humbug's most recent victims used to live no longer displayed any evidence of the savageries committed there. But Scrooge knew it instantly, and his mind easily replaced the vanished bloodstains and removed corpses in place of the current occupant's furniture, appliances, and holiday decorations as he walked from room to room.

It was a large two-story house situated on a street of similar homes in Northgate, a neighborhood historically important for being the site of the first covered shopping mall in the United States. Scrooge paused at a wall of framed photographs, the people smiling back from beneath the glass strangers to him—*living* strangers. Slowly, however, the images changed and he saw the deceased family as he'd found them one year ago, their ugly mutilations and bizarre poses preserved in his mind as fixedly as in any of Oliver's crime scene photos.

In the faces of the corpses he saw the other families claimed by Humbug: their homes, appliances, and holiday decorations. He saw their framed photos and watched as their smiles stretched into silent screams that would never end. Each family destroyed by a homicidal maniac as part of some strange desecration of an otherwise wholesome holiday.

The catalogue of violations and indignities inflicted on Humbug's victims ran through Scrooge's mind unbidden. It was a ponderous mental burden, more so even than Scrooge had realized for some time, resignedly accustomed to it as he'd become. He moved shakily to the sofa and collapsed, unaware that Zodiac had appeared beside him until the spirit spoke.

"If you are going to catch your killer before they up their score again you'd better get off your ass and do something. How were they chosen, Detective? What attracts this particular predator to such quarry?"

"I don't know."

"Guess."

"We've been through all this. The profiles and diagnostics didn't help. Even Marley, brilliant as she was, and all the best shrinks in the F.B.I. couldn't settle on anything definite. There isn't enough evidence."

"Humbug's restraint is his strength. If he killed more often, you'd have better clues. His opportunities to make a mistake are scarce."

"You might put it that way," Scrooge said, remembering his own words to Marley on their final Christmas Eve together. "Trust me, nothing connects the families except they all lived in the general Seattle area and were all murdered and there's nothing I can do about it."

"Houses."

"What?"

"They all lived in houses in the general Seattle area. No apartments or condos. No townhomes. No trailer parks. No houseboats."

"So? They were all spoiled wealthy suburbanites, who cares?"

"It's very noisy work, torturing somebody to death. Believe me, I know. He needs some degree of privacy to spend such a great deal of uninterrupted time with his victims. Personally, I found it much more thrilling to strike quickly and disappear. But your man likes to linger. To each his own, I suppose."

"We already crosschecked workers and delivery people who might have been to all five areas. Nothing came of it."

The letters and sigils on Zodiac's paper skin seemed to flicker as if lit from within by candles. The blazes of his eyes appeared freshly stoked, the flames heartier. Tiny wafts of smoke curled up from his seams and cracks. The scent of burning was stronger.

"They all celebrated Christmas."

Now, Scrooge was angry. He stood, gesturing around the room as he shouted, "No shit, asshole! They all celebrated Christmas. They all had too much money, shopped at snobby specialty stores, took overseas vacations, and sent their precious brats to pampered private schools. Look, I don't *like* these people, okay? I admit that. But none of them ever hurt anyone and they didn't deserve what they got."

"Interesting," Zodiac mused. *"Seems your killer has a definite type."*

"It's almost creepy," Scrooge said. "After the first two, even I started to get déjà vu walking into every new crime scene. You're damn right they were similar, right down to the organic oat milk in their smart refrigerators. They all drove the same luxury cars and had the best of everything money could buy. They also all had door frames where they marked their kids' height once a year and the exact same goddamn family portraits on their walls with everyone smiling and dressed in their Sunday best. Who does that?"

Scrooge became silent and looked intently at the wall of photographs.

"Penny for your thoughts, Detective?"

"Nothing. If it was worth seeing, Marley would have seen it. She was the smart one. The chief was right to take me off the case. I'm too old and tired and I don't want to be in this room anymore.

Show me something happy, you perverted pile of garbage. Show me one single good thing about this fucking holiday."

Zodiac brought his hands together in a thunderous clap and the whole world began to spin. The decorative lights strung around the living room burned painfully bright. Scrooge shielded his eyes and tried to turn away but tripped over the coffee table beside the sofa. He tumbled toward the floor and collapsed onto—

—sand.

Warm and soft.

A beach.

Exactly the kind of pristine and picturesque stretch of snow-white sand most people only see on calendars and screensavers. The sky overhead was an impossibly flawless shade of blue, unmarred by a single cloud. Scrooge felt sunshine warm his skin and the tickling caress of a refreshing tropical breeze, heard the murmuring of gentle waves in the background. He looked up and found himself contemplating a vast expanse of the ocean. He saw people reveling in the surf and, further away, swimmers dotted the glittering water's surface. Slowly, he turned.

The young woman lying on a towel beneath a big pink umbrella at first looked too mature to be his daughter, and Scrooge had the eerie sensation life had somehow sped up around him.

But no, it was Ellen.

Of course he'd known she wasn't a little girl anymore, he was not quite that far out of touch. Ellen was a college freshman, after all. Scrooge recalled the last time he'd seen his daughter: dutifully helping her new roommate move boxes into their dorm room on a sweaty Sunday back in August. It wasn't really so long ago, he thought. But she'd cut her dark brown hair much shorter since, and her black bikini (skimpier than he'd have liked) showed off the beginnings of an intricate flower-print tattoo on her left thigh, which looked fairly fresh. He opened his mouth—to say what? Scrooge had no idea—then closed it again.

"A wise decision, Detective. I'd hate to think you were that tedious."

Scrooge whirled about, his hand going to the holster and gun he was not wearing, and found Zodiac lounging on a canvas beach chair, hands behind his head. Somewhere, he'd acquired a pair of mirrored sunglasses that hid the conflagrations of his eyes. But the fire within him was clearly growing and licked at his papery hide with many tiny tongues of flame. The smoke coming off him was getting thicker, darker, more pungent.

"Hot enough for you?" Scrooge asked.

Zodiac giggled and Scrooge suppressed a shudder. The ringing of Ellen's phone brought Scrooge's attention back to his daughter as she answered, "Hi, Mom."

"I said show me something *happy*," Scrooge grumbled over his shoulder. "My ex-wife makes me the opposite of happy."

"Women," Zodiac sighed, *"I hear you. Can't live with them, can't possibly stockpile enough copper-jacketed bullets to kill them all. Still, I feel obligated to point out in my own defense that I do not see your ex-wife here, do you?"*

"Now who's tedious?"

Ellen was absently dragging one finger through the sand as she spoke. "Still at the beach... Same spot, yeah... No, I didn't forget...

Because I don't really want to get to know your new boyfriend...
Well, just tell Gary—*Harry*, sorry... I said I'm sorry, didn't I?"

"Who the hell is Harry?" Scrooge asked.

"How about I meet you guys there?" A long moment passed,
and Scrooge took some small satisfaction in watching his
daughter roll her eyes. "Yeah, fine," she said at last. "Look,
Mom, I know you don't want to hear this but Dad's still not
answering his phone... A couple of times... Because I'm worried
about him, aren't you?"

"Dumb question," muttered Scrooge.

"It is not!" Ellen said. "It's not the same thing at all. You know
what he's dealing with right now. Yes, he's angry and unpleasant
and I wasn't exactly upset about the idea of spending Christmas
a few thousand miles away from him this year, but that doesn't
mean we shouldn't check on him, does it? I mean, it's Christmas for him too, you know? Why doesn't he answer?"

His daughter's final question rang in Scrooge's head like the
echoing of church bells in an otherwise silent morning.

Why doesn't he answer?

He heard it again and again, each time louder, more echoing.
Ellen's voice changed with each repetition, grew deeper and
more insistent, as the world spun around him. Scrooge lost
sight of his daughter and fought to keep his balance.

Why doesn't he answer?

The ocean and sky switched places and bled into each other,
like a freshly finished painting left out in the rain, as Scrooge
fell headlong into the cool blue abyss.

Why doesn't—

"—he answer?" Detective Bobby Alwyn said. "I've tried four times already."

A woman's voice responded, but Scrooge was too disoriented to follow what she said. He slowly realized the blue void was actually a ceiling. The feeling of carpet beneath him led Scrooge to understand he was lying on his back on the floor of Bobby's apartment. A small place, but orderly and tastefully appointed.

Scrooge got up and looked around, taking in the tiny fake Christmas tree on a footstool, several brightly wrapped packages assembled beneath it. Three black-and-white landscape photographs in simple wood frames hung about the room. From within the small brick fireplace blazed a fire that completed the cozy holiday mood. Near it was a plush sofa on which Bobby and a pretty dark-haired young woman Scrooge recognized, but could not immediately place, sat together. She was drinking a glass of red wine, Bobby a mug of coffee.

"I just can't understand why you care so much," the woman said. And it was the slight hint of Southern accent in her voice that aided Scrooge's recognition. She was a paramedic with whom he and Bobby often crossed paths at crime scenes. "Everybody knows Scrooge is a major asshole."

Don't call me that, Scrooge thought, trying to remember the woman's name. *Layla, perhaps? Maybe Lyla or Laurie? Good job, detective. Way to take note of things.*

"Please, Lyla, I've asked you not to call him that." Even as he spoke, though, Bobby couldn't help but laugh. "He really, really hates it."

Scrooge wondered how long the two had been seeing each other. Something about the apartment, orderly as it was, left Scrooge convinced it was the residence of a bachelor, although the paramedic looked right at home on the sofa in her loose sweat pants and oversized Seattle Kraken shirt. Theirs was clearly not a budding relationship, so why hadn't Bobby said anything to him about it?

Why the hell would he? What opening did you give him? What interest did you show?

Lyla slowly rubbed her thumb and middle finger together. "Just for Scrooge," she said. "A special Christmas Eve solo by the World's Smallest Violin."

Bobby snorted and nearly choked as he drank from his steaming mug. He was dressed in dark jeans and white Seattle Police Department polo shirt, and though he looked exhausted he also exhibited the body language of somebody clearly about to leave, perhaps in a rush.

Of course, thought Scrooge, who'd spent all of his own recent Christmas Eves similarly on edge. *There's a crime scene in his future. Another vicious blood-soaked Christmas present from Humbug. He knows the call is coming, but not exactly when.*

"You're always defending him," Lyla placed a hand on Bobby's thigh. "I'm afraid you're going to get hurt."

"The only person he really hurts is himself. How he is, it drives people away, sure, but he's the one depressed by it. His marriage flamed out, his only kid avoids him, and who suffers most? Who's alone at Christmas? It's him. He's obviously a smart guy, but again and again he uses his fists instead of his brain like some Hollywood cliché. And who gets booted off the case? It's him! He's not a villain, you know? He's just kind of... Pathetic, I guess is the word."

"You got that right," Lyla said. "The old guy has 'self-inflicted gunshot' written all over him. Either that or he'll self-destruct on the job somehow. You can't get too attached or you'll end up going down with him."

A large portion of the fire extracted itself from the hearth and stood. A figure made of flame. Zodiac spread his arms wide in a kind of lazy stretch, his voice somehow unaffected by the slow-motion incineration of his body.

"My time grows short."

"Are spirits' lives really that brief?" asked Scrooge.

"My time allotted to visit this plane is very brief. Tomorrow will bring a new crop of horror and crime out of which I'll be reborn yet again. There are rules, Detective. Soon I must entrust you to another and return to... Well, perhaps it's best you don't know. Not yet. Ignore tonight's lessons and you'll find out for yourself soon enough. Either way, my realm is the present. The world of tomorrow is not my purview."

"I'll be careful, I promise." Bobby took Lyla's hand. "But Detective Caine is a good man under all the tough guy bullshit and bullying. He lost somebody very important to him last year and now he's lost his mission, too. I know how that feels. What he's going through, I wouldn't wish it on anybody."

"Bobby, you can't compare yourself to him. It's a totally different situation with Scroo—sorry, with good ol' Detective Caine. You were in the Army. Military combat in Afghanistan is not the same thing at all. That was war."

"So is this." Bobby moved to kneel beside the small tree and began examining the decorated packages on the floor.

"I didn't even know the kid was a vet," Scrooge said. "He never mentioned anything about it."

"What interest did you show?"

"You're right. I guess I never really gave him any kind of chance. Didn't bother getting to know him much. Tell me, how bad is tomorrow going to be for him?"

"My realm is the present, Detective. Have you forgotten the meanings of the word?"

"No," Scrooge said softly. "I didn't forget."

"Growing up," Bobby said, "we were always allowed to open one gift on Christmas Eve. I want to enjoy whatever part of this holiday I can with you while there's still time. And I got something here with your name on it. So tell me, have you been a good girl this year?"

Lyla raised her glass. "As good as gold and better."

Bobby frowned. "I'm sorry to hear that, babe. Because this particular Santa only gives presents to naughty girls." He gently shook the package. "Shame, because I think you would have really liked this."

"Oh no." Lyla winked as she lay back on the couch and began to untie the strings knotted at the waist of her pants. "Guess it's a good thing I still have a few hours left to change my ways, huh?"

"So fortunate."

"Come here, Santa. I'll sit on your lap and show you just how naughty I can be."

Scrooge looked away as the couple entwined on the couch and saw Zodiac form a pistol with his flaming thumb and forefinger, then aim it at them.

"Ah, young love. But how much more alluring would she be hogtied and screaming?"

"Cut the shit," Scrooge said. "Message received. I get it, okay? I can't let this case destroy Bobby and he's going to need help. My ego doesn't matter anymore. I'll do whatever I can to assist him, even quit the force and work the case freelance if I have to. And I'm going to make things right with Ellen. I'll call her back tonight, right after you take me home. Do the magic teleportation bit now, please. Mission accomplished."

Zodiac wrapped his fiery arms around Scrooge in a scorching hug.

"Alas, Detective, if only it were so easy."

Fire spread and rose around them as Scrooge screamed and struggled, his nose filling with the scent of his own burning flesh. An enormous blaze consumed him, Zodiac, the room, Bobby and Lyla—the whole world. The very fabric of reality itself seemed to blacken and curl like shredded scraps of paper tossed into the hottest pit of Inferno.

"We've one visit left to pay before our time ends," Zodiac whispered. *"The final present."*

The city of Port Orchard was most easily reached from downtown Seattle by ferry. A faster passenger-only boat was available during certain times of year, but otherwise the nearly hour-long passage on a standard state vessel, which also transported vehicles, from Seattle's Colman Dock to the terminal in the nearby city of Bremerton was the typical traveler's route.

From there it was a short drive into the heart of Port Orchard. The governmental seat of Kitsap County was rechristened as such long ago in honor of a revered leader of the Suquamish Tribe, Chief Kitsap, said to have been at one time the most powerful tribal leader in the Puget Sound region.

Before that, it had been known as Slaughter County.

Beyond being the base of operations for various local governmental institutions, the city of Port Orchard was largely residential, home to commuters who traveled into the neighboring cities of Silverdale and Bremerton, or all the way to Seattle, for work. Ironically, one of its more famous residents was actress Karolyn Grimes, best known for her role as young Zuzu Bailey in Frank Capra's 1946 film *It's A Wonderful Life*. A movie Annabelle Hewitt loved, but Detective Stewart Caine had never seen, despite her urging. Although, to be fair, he was nearly always disinterested in any film that did not star Clint Eastwood, Steven Seagal, or Angie Dickinson.

Also, something about the concept of guardian angels would not have sat especially well with a man obligated to immerse himself in so many incidents of senseless depravity and violence.

Yes, it's fair to say that Scrooge would have some rather serious questions for the wingless Clarence Odbody about his bosses, and the methods of the detective's interrogation would likely have left the funny little fellow in serious doubt about his mission to protect and assist humanity. In the right (or wrong) mood, as had often been said in hushed tones around Seattle P.D. headquarters, old Scrooge could even scare an angel.

And such was *exactly* Detective Caine's mood as he watched the scene unfolding before him, a tragedy in the making if he'd ever seen one—and he most certainly had.

Tim Hewitt was a boy in his early teens, thin and sickly looking at the best of times. He'd spent the last few hours riding his bike in the day's increasingly wet and cold weather and it had left him downright wan and clearly exhausted. Scrooge, helplessly pulled along in the boy's wake, was forced to watch as he went about making surreptitious deliveries of small unlabeled packages and padded envelopes, hurriedly exchanging them for tightly folded wads of money at various sketchy parking lots and bus stops. The detective's specialty was homicide, but he knew a drug deal when he saw one. And Tim's employer was a renowned scumbag familiar to every cop in the Pacific Northwest.

As Tim shifted nervously in the living room of Jasper Sikes, the man for whom he'd been making the deliveries, the boy's breathing was ragged and strained, relief slow to come even after several uses of his inhaler.

What Scrooge could see of the dirty and cluttered house fit with what he knew of its owner. Takeout containers and empty beer cans were collected into small piles here and there on the floor. One wall was dominated by a huge flatscreen television, likely stolen. The only other aspect of the place not neglected or filthy was a collection of swords, all made famous in movies and TV shows, displayed on the wall above an aquarium. Inside, a large python lay perfectly motionless beneath a heat lamp. With the television off, it was the brightest source of light in the room.

A painfully skinny white guy of about thirty, with a short patchy beard and long stringy hair so greasy it might have been most recently washed last Christmas Eve, his milky skin heavily inked with sloppy prison tattoos, Jasper sat at a plastic table in the adjacent kitchen, hunched over the cash Tim had brought him.

"Stop wheezing or wait outside." He glanced up from the money spread on the table. "You're screwing up my count and you look like shit."

Jasper wore a dingy T-shirt which had once been white, freckled with tiny holes where cigarette ashes had fallen onto it, fraying basketball shorts, and black Crocs. His eyes were markedly different shades of blue and green, which gave his already menacing glare an especially unsettling effect.

Finished at last, he counted out Tim's fee and slid the bills across the table.

"Told you it was all there." Tim rushed to collect his pay before retreating again to stand further away from Jasper's cloud of smoke and near as possible to the door. "Why'd you hire me if you don't trust me?"

"I trust nobody, kid," Jasper sneered around his cigarette. "And I hired you because you look good and pathetic. The kind of sad little loser nobody remembers."

Tim said nothing as he pocketed the money, stifling a cough. Scrooge could see the smoke was bothering the boy. Jasper saw it too and blew a smelly gray cloud pointedly in Tim's direction.

"Your mom home?"

"Soon."

"Where do you tell her you get the cash?"

"I don't tell her anything."

Jasper nodded, lighting another cigarette on the smoldering filter of the last. "How many dicks you think she sucked in her life?"

Tim reached for the door. "Text me when you're ready again. School doesn't start back up until after the first."

"Don't be like that, kid. I thought we were buddies. So what if your mom's a hot slut? It's not your fault. And I'm just messing with you. Seriously, though, how many guys you think have put it in her ass? Double digits for sure, right?"

Scrooge felt a surge of rage in his chest so intense that it gave him pause. It was gruesome to contemplate what he might have done to the dealer had he actually been in the room. Contemplate it he did, however. Scrooge thought it over carefully and felt a smile tugging at the corners of his mouth.

Tim paused, his hand on the knob, and said, "I know one guy who never will."

"Fuck you!" Jasper brayed with laughter, slamming his palms onto the cheap table. "You sickly wheezing little retard. Maybe next time I get somebody else for the job? How'd you like that?"

"And maybe next time Detective Caine asks me how things are going I mention the pervy felon next door asked me to help him deal drugs. How'd you like that?"

Jasper's laughter died a quick brutal death in his throat.

"Don't threaten me, kid. Not even as a joke. I may need your help for now, while I'm still on probation, but nobody talks to me like that. Besides, I know that geezer hasn't been around in a long time. He took your mommy to pound town, hit that shit and quit it, you understand? He won't help you. And if you ever think about telling somebody about our arrangement, it won't matter how many cops you cry to. Kids disappear every day in this world. Believe me, faggot. For your own good."

Jasper stood, opened the refrigerator, and took out a can of beer. "Now get lost. I got people coming over to watch *Die Hard*."

Scrooge followed the boy outside, down the short rickety steps from the front door of Jasper's house to his weed-choked front yard, and onto the sidewalk. Tim began to unchain his bike from a telephone pole when a fit of harsh coughing nearly brought him to his knees. Night had fallen and the snow was coming down more heavily.

As Tim struggled with his inhaler, a slim blackened shape crept out from behind the pole, almost sheepishly. Zodiac was little more than a charred skeleton whose bones were too thin and unnaturally long. Nightmare physiology designed by a lunatic god. His proportions necessitated strange halting movements, jerks and spasms, as he wobbled and tottered his way into the light.

"Tell me, Spirit," said Scrooge, watching as Tim began to recover, "will the boy be okay?"

"Tomorrow is the realm of a different specter. But I do see a vacancy. His bicycle, neglected and starting to rust. His inhaler buried in a drawer. And a very lonely woman in the house beyond."

Zodiac pointed one trembling hand toward a neat blue one-story behind a row of snow-capped hedges, dark for the moment and empty.

"Then again, I don't know why you care. You aren't interested in playing house with some sad single mom and her sickly brat. Just because you fucked her a few times, that doesn't mean the silly bitch needs to start picking out matching pajamas for the whole happy family."

Tim walked his bicycle across the street, breathing noisily but better, and parked it just inside the open door of a small attached garage before going inside. Scrooge followed, leaving the skeleton of Zodiac clumsily stumbling after him. Pieces of the spirit's scorched bones began flaking off under the force of the cold wind, dancing away like blackened snowflakes into the night.

Scrooge was familiar enough with the house and found his way around without much thought, watching as Tim went to his bedroom—the typically messy domain of a teenage boy: floor littered with clothes and every inch of wall occupied by posters of either bands Scrooge didn't recognize or anime characters—and stashed most of the money he'd earned in an old sneaker hidden under his desk. He took the rest and went into his mother's room.

This space, Scrooge knew well. It was where he'd spent the majority of visits to the house and it hadn't changed since his last trip. Like her office, Belle's bedroom was clean but cluttered. A strange mix of kitsch and class was in evidence on either side of her canopy bed, the curtains of which were semi-transparent, pink, adorned with a pattern of red musical notes.

There were too many pieces of furniture for a room this size, including several antique dressers and three mismatched old chairs of various clashing styles—all rummage sale finds, Scrooge knew, which Belle had been unable to resist. She frequented flea markets and secondhand shops with a strange kind of intensity, being a sucker for vintage clothes, retro furniture, and fixer-uppers of all types. It was a predilection about which she'd teased Scrooge multiple times: *What's that say about why I like you, old man?*

Scrooge watched Tim pull out the bottom drawer of one particularly old chest and remove a metal lunchbox, the label on which was faded beyond recognition. He put the bills inside, being careful to fold them in among the money already there. It looked to Scrooge to be no small amount.

Of course, he thought. *The boy knows what it's like to leave someplace in a hurry and take only what you can carry. He knows the value of keeping cash on hand. He understands how quickly things can go bad.*

As Tim hurried to leave the room, his cough having returned with a vengeance and his inhaler sitting out of reach, Zodiac, or what little remained of him, entered. Tiny pieces of his scorched skeleton fell away with every movement, like grains of sand escaping a fist. The now-empty caves of his eye sockets regarded Scrooge (or perhaps they didn't) but his newly revealed mouth seemed somehow friendly, despite its lack of lips.

"Got to be the only teenager in the world sneaking money *into* his mom's emergency stash," Scrooge said. "He knows what it's like to have nothing. He's been there before. Christ, I never meant to say he wasn't a good kid. Can you see if... Do you think there's a chance he might be okay?"

"Tomorrow is the realm—"

"Of a different specter, yeah right. Maybe it's time I finally meet this farsighted friend of yours, huh?"

"Oh, rest assured that your final guide is no friend of mine."

Zodiac shuddered, bracing himself against the wall as his bones continued, more rapidly now, disintegrating. He gestured, as much as his crumbling arm would allow, toward the house's front door.

"A servant of oblivion. They are relentless, without nostalgia or sympathy. Unrestrained by expectations, necessity, or conscience. These are the fundamental hallmarks of the Future itself, and also its avatar. The one who now awaits your arrival."

Scrooge's departure was halted by an eruption of ghastly cackling from the deteriorating spirit. But the detective found, when he turned to share in the joke, nothing but a scattering of ink-black ash on the carpet and the faint scent of smoke and sulfur. The unsettling certainty that he was, despite appearances, still not alone.

He passed Tim's bedroom, the boy inside now and safe for the moment, presumably awaiting the return of his mother later that night to make lasagna and watch a movie, and marched boldly through Belle's front door without opening it.

The steadily falling snow had been replaced by a cloud of low fog so thick as to make the world unnavigable. In no more than four or five steps Scrooge lost sight of the house, of the entire neighborhood, and walked blindly in the swirling mist. For how long he wandered, he could not say. He didn't brush against anything, sense any obstacles, and he felt no change in the flat stony ground underfoot as he stumbled onward, directionless.

Then, finally, there was something new.

A sound. *Tap.*

Sharp and metallic, like a chisel piercing stone. *Tap.*

Tap! Each strike distinct and growing louder, coming closer. A distant brightness from some unseen source appeared through the mist, giving Scrooge a definite course to follow.

Tap! Tap!! Tap!!!

Silhouetted by the alien light, a figure came slowly through the murky gloom. Leaning jauntily on a cane, they paused as if enjoying a leisurely stroll through some far more pleasant landscape.

"Of course," Scrooge said. "I should have guessed."

Tall and lean, wearing a top hat and draped in a long flowing cloak with a high collar, the figure preceded its advance with another decisive strike of their cane on the ground. It was this cadence which Scrooge had heard, each new strike growing louder as he and the third, final spirit drew cautiously closer to one another.

"Jack the Ripper, I presume."

Slowly, almost elegantly, the spirit reached up with one gloved hand and tipped their hat.

STAVE FOUR

STRAIGHT OUTTA WHITECHAPEL (CHRISTMAS FUTURE)

Jack the Ripper was an unidentified serial killer active in and around the impoverished Whitechapel district of London, England, in 1888... Attacks ascribed to Jack the Ripper typically involved women working as prostitutes who lived and worked in the slums of the East End of London. Their throats were cut prior to abdominal mutilations. The removal of internal organs from at least three of the victims led to speculation that their killer had some anatomical or surgical knowledge. Rumors that the murders were connected intensified in September and October 1888, and numerous letters were received by media outlets and Scotland Yard from individuals purporting to be the murderer... The murders were never solved, and the legends surrounding these crimes became a combination of historical research, folklore, and pseudohistory, capturing public imagination to the present day.

– Wikipedia

Jack was a *woman*.

Closer now, separated only by faint wisps of fog, Scrooge took more thorough stock of his last ghostly guide. What he could see of the notorious killer left no doubt; the cloak, fastened tightly at Jack's slender throat with an ornate gold clasp, fell open to reveal a decidedly feminine form beneath.

A bone-white corset, barely containing an ample bust, was cinched tightly at her waist, just above a wide bell-shaped skirt the color of fresh blood on concrete, which extended to the ground and obscured the wearer's feet. The movements beneath were unsettlingly odd, there appeared to be too many legs at work, each far too long and skinny. Rather than bending at the knee, as normal, the spirit's hidden limbs seemed to almost curl, propelling Jack forward in the eerie slithering manner of some gliding reptile. Only the sound of the cane's measured tapping gave the spirit's advancement the illusion of more typical bipedal locomotion. Watching Jack move sent ripples of fear through Scrooge's heart, though he could not say exactly why.

But the Ripper's face? Somehow, that was even worse.

Beneath the hat, curtains of hair so black it almost looked to be tinted blue framed the upper portion of a sharp angular countenance, one whose bloodlessly white skin was impossibly devoid of lines or blemishes. The spirit's eyes were large and round, their pupils a brilliant shade of violet freckled with dots of amber. There was malevolence to be read in those eyes, Scrooge thought, and passion, as well as a dreadful capacity for patience on a scale unimaginable to normal human beings.

Beneath the sharp nose, the rest of Jack's face was hidden behind a carefully wrapped crimson scarf. As Scrooge looked her over, Jack's eyes gleamed with some hidden, private amusement. Finally, she raised one hand, sheathed in an immaculately white evening glove, and waved with all of her long thin fingers.

"I take it," Scrooge said at last, "you are the Ghost of Christmas Yet to Come?"

Jack did not answer beyond a flash of glee in her mesmerizing eyes, then gestured wordlessly onward with a sweep of her cane. After the grandiose proclamations of the Butcher, and Zodiac's sarcastic antagonism, Jack's silence was unexpectedly terrifying. Scrooge found he was unable to move and could not tear his gaze from Jack's.

Without the option for his normal response of physical intimidation (he could not imagine a course of action that would earn more than bemused indifference from the being before him) and with the spirit being unable (or unwilling) to engage in conversation, unpleasant as it was sure to be, the detective found himself seeking solace in the process of deduction. Once upon a time such reasoning, as taught to him by an old pro, had brought comfort to the chaotic and trauma-filled life of the young boy he'd been. Scrooge flexed his atrophied mental muscles of observation and speculation and considered all three spirits again.

The Mad Butcher of Kingsbury Run, who'd preyed on the most hopeless members of an already disadvantaged community, one plagued by crime, disease, and soul-crushing poverty, was revealed in the afterlife as the disgusting scavenger he always was. A human parasite, more maggot than man, and so full of perversity it literally came leaking from his empty eyes in the form of nauseating pus.

Likewise, having been exiled to his own less-than-great hereafter, Zodiac was exposed as the weak and pitiful sadist he'd truly been. Utterly empty, the merest skeleton of a human, he was ultimately shown to be completely without substance when not cocooned inside the headlines he tried so desperately to inspire. There was nothing much to him beyond the evidence of his crimes, which he was now forced to watch incinerate and disappear anew each and every day for all time.

Jack's personification, however, merited more thorough consideration.

The world's most notorious unidentified serial murderer was thought by some experts to have been a woman: a psychopathic midwife, perhaps, judging from the killer's apparent knowledge of anatomy, or maybe the blood-crazed purveyor of illicit back-alley abortions. Scrooge felt certain there was something awful waiting to be revealed beneath the fiend's costume. Her skirt and scarf might hide the true extent of her spiritual metamorphosis, but was the murderer's appearance confirmation of the theory regarding the Ripper's actual gender? Or was it simply a further degree of cosmic penance for Jack to be forced to spend eternity trapped in the very form he'd tried so passionately to mutilate and obliterate beyond recognition?

As if reading Scrooge's thoughts all too plainly, Jack's sole response was the merest arching of one eyebrow as, once again, she indicated their path with her cane.

"You're going to show me things that have not happened yet, but will happen in the future," Scrooge said. "Am I right?"

Jack's head nodded once, but the killer gave no other reply save to glide ahead on her strange unseen legs, then pause and look back, clearly expecting Scrooge to follow. But still his feet would not obey the detective's mental command to move.

Jack began impatiently tapping the ground with her cane.

"I'm sorry, Jack." Scrooge forced the words from a throat tight with panic, his mouth painfully dry, tongue suddenly thick and clumsy. "I'm afraid to see what happens next. You're here to help, I know that. Marley said so, and she has no reason to lie. I understand the point of all this, I know how the original story goes, and do I want to repair my life—really, I do. But could you please just say something? Anything?"

The Ripper beckoned Scrooge forward with one finger.

"Alright," Scrooge gasped, "I'm coming."

And he moved at last, one slow deliberate step after another. "Time's a-wasting, I suppose." Scrooge's voice was strained and childlike, unrecognizable to himself. *Was this madness?* "Marley was right when she said there are lives at stake—and souls, too. And not just mine, I know that now. Lead on, Jack. I'll follow and I'll see whatever you have to show me. Do your worst. I'm scared, but I'm coming. I'm ready."

The Ripper moved away exactly as she'd arrived, in the same smooth slithering motion, back through the dense fog and toward the ghostly source of the faraway light. Scrooge followed in her shadow, which seemingly hefted him up, or so he imagined, and carried him along.

❧ ⸱⸱◆⸱⸱ ❧

They did not so much enter the room as the room seemed to materialize around them. Vague forms at first, dimly visible through the mist, and echoing sound of indistinct voices. The scene quickly grew solid and substantial until the fog was completely gone, the light replaced with a large brightly glowing TV screen, and Scrooge found himself back inside the squalid home of Jasper Sikes.

Lounging around the room, slouched on the sofa and sprawled on the floor, was a small group of shady characters, several known to Scrooge as local delinquents, thieves, and repeat petty offenders. The air was thick with the reek of pot as they smoked and drank and stared at the TV, where a boy named Kevin, in anticipation of an impending robbery, set booby traps in various places around an immense suburban mansion.

A fat man with a wispy neck beard seated at one end of the sofa looked up from noisily sucking at a bong and said, "Weird to think how that kid's dead now."

On the floor, a thin woman with short strawberry blonde hair and numerous facial piercings looked up from dividing lines of coke on a wooden cutting board. "He isn't dead," she snapped. "Dude was just in *American Horror Story*."

"No," the fat man shook his head, "that was another guy. This kid died way back in the nineties."

"Macaulay Culkin is not dead." The woman lowered her face to the white powder and snorted two lines.

"Then who OD'd in that nightclub hanging out with Johnny Depp?"

Jasper appeared in the kitchen doorway, a can of beer in one hand, his arm around a snickering girl far too young for such company and indulgences, saying, "You're thinking of the kid from *Stand By Me*. Now shut the fuck up, Bennie, I like this part."

On screen, one of the thieves wrapped his hand around a doorknob, searing his flesh on the blazing-hot metal, and screamed. Everybody in the room laughed—except Bennie. Absently flicking his lighter, looking with stoned intensity at the tiny flame as it winked in and out of life, the fat man languidly mused, "I guess you would be the expert on the subject of dead kids."

A chilly silence fell over the room. Jasper pushed aside his underage companion and stalked to the sofa, his empty hand forming into a fist. "What did you just say to me? Say it again, Bennie. Go ahead, you fuck. Say that shit one more time."

Bennie glanced around the room with obvious confusion, looking for help and finding none in the smirking faces around him. Their eyes shone, clearly excited by the prospect of blood being shed. Bennie's mouth hung open stupidly, as if even his tongue couldn't believe the words he'd just spoken, while on TV the assault of Kevin's home continued. The big man mumbled, weakly fumbling for some kind of response that might avoid the violence that seemed an inevitable part of his immediate future.

"One word," Jasper whispered. "Just one word, Bennie, and I'll break your fat fucking face."

Slowly, Bennie lowered his gaze to the floor. Turning to the room, talking over the noise of the TV, Jasper said, "I don't want to hear another word about that kid, you got it? I fucking told him what to do if he got spotted: play dumb and say he found the shit he was carrying. How many times did I tell him? Clarissa, don't I tell you the exact same thing?"

The teenage girl nodded behind a bottle of hard lemonade, eager to please.

"Goddamn right, I do. Dead kids are bad for business, you morons. I've had cops on my ass since he bought it. My parole officer is super pissed. That wheezing little sissy had no business running from anyone, let alone the cops. And if he hadn't been more afraid of disappointing his slut mommy than he was of getting caught, he'd still be alive. It's not my fault."

Jasper smacked the bong out of Bennie's shaking hands. "I said it's not my fault!"

In the corner, near the python terrarium, Scrooge watched the scene in silence. The snake had raised its head in Jack's direction, forked tongue tasting the air as if the creature somehow sensed the ghost's presence. But a sharp glance from the spirit sent the snake quickly into hiding beneath a thick branch.

Scrooge saw Jasper return to the kitchen, take Clarissa by the hand and lead her down a short hallway toward what he presumed was the bedroom. Only then did the others slowly, cautiously, resume their intoxicated banter—all except Bennie. The big man's eyes stayed on the floor, his mouth slightly open, his eyes blank with lingering shock. To the mute specter with the smiling eyes, Scrooge said, "Tell me, Jack, are these the shadows of things that *will* be, or things that only *might* be?"

Beyond the slight twitching of her face beneath the blood-colored scarf, the Ripper made no reply.

"I really don't understand why you would bother to show me all this if it was too late for me to do anything about it. There must still be time, right?"

Jack glided to the TV and smartly rapped the screen with her cane. Instantly, Jasper's guests froze and the picture changed. Scrooge saw Belle's office at Tailfeathers, the delightfully tacky furnishings all the more familiar and welcoming for how long it felt since he'd last been there. Unthinkable, how drastically things had changed since he'd spoken so harshly to Belle in that place!

She was alone and sitting at the desk, head in her hands, crying. Scrooge wondered at his absence from the scene. Surely, he thought, there was no way he'd leave her alone at such a time? Not if her son had really just died? But, reticent to turn the focus of the moment onto himself and nagged by a vague and indistinct fear he could not articulate (or perhaps did not want to), he said nothing.

Maybe, he thought, *there's a good reason I'm not there?*

At last, the slowly growing pressure in his chest threatening to explode, Scrooge, thinking the odds very good that if he began to cry he might never be able to stop, looked away from the TV. He turned and found himself in a completely different room, one he did not recognize.

Only the butchered corpses were familiar.

But they were enough.

A crime scene. Location of the latest Humbug murder, Scrooge knew the maniac's grisly handiwork when he saw it. He moved forward for a closer look, tripping on the trio of carpeted stairs which led down into the slightly sunken room. It was an odd place for stairs; some holdover, maybe, from the era in which the house was originally designed? Too expensive or bothersome to renovate? Scrooge, having no interest in architecture or interior decoration, recovered himself and walked to the corner, studying the scene as he went.

It was the living room of another spacious suburban home. The residence of another comfortable family, their tastefully understated holiday decorations a bizarre compliment to the elaborately atrocious states in which their bodies had been left.

Standing beside the detective, Jack the Ripper's excitement over the brutality on display was practically palpable. The ghostly murderer swayed gently back and forth, like a famished cobra eyeing an overweight rat, all of her long slender fingers wrapped so tightly around her cane that the white fabric of her gloves strained at the seams.

Both parents were on the sofa, their naked corpses missing large pieces; trophies, no doubt, which Scrooge expected to be found either wrapped in bright paper and nestled under the tree, or inside the four stockings hung on the mantle. The older child, a boy whose short hair only accented his unfortunately large ears, was on the floor, completely dismembered.

Scrooge finally dragged his eyes away from the grisly tableau after briefly examining the youngest child, a girl with long dark hair, who'd been gutted so savagely as to be nearly cut in half, then strung up on the tree like some kind of repulsive angel.

A bay of immense windows in the room's far wall looked out over a yard full of illuminated figures. On TV, a fireplace crackled cheerfully. Scrooge watched as two C.S.I. technicians clad in blue jumpsuits, their shoes wrapped in plastic, gloved hands carrying boxy black cases full of equipment, walked in from the entryway.

Both of them stumbled on the stairs.

Moments later, Detective Bobby Alwyn followed, and he also tripped on the stairs, very nearly falling straight into the mutilated remains of the boy.

He appeared older, more tired, his mustache had spread over his face and became a short beard, the previously dark hair now shot through with silver. It was difficult to say exactly how far into the future this moment was, though it clearly was not Bobby's first in-person exposure to one of Humbug's gruesome "gifts." He went about the scene with the weary resignation of somebody grown accustomed to such obscenities. Scrooge knew the look very well.

Beside the sofa was a table on which, leaning against a delicate glass lamp, rested a Christmas card. On the front was a Rockwellian scene of two children overjoyed about the adorable puppy bursting out of a brightly wrapped box with a big red bow on its head. Inside, Scrooge knew, would be another untraceable taunt from the killer.

Oliver Drood entered without a word, two large cameras hanging around his neck, shoes also wrapped in protective plastic. He smoothly descended the stairs without pause.

"Did you see that?" Scrooge asked. "He knew about the stairs."

Jack's eyes glinted, but she said nothing.

"He's been here before." Scrooge went quickly to the wall opposite the windows and looked over the framed photographs on display there. In the center, a large family portrait: everyone smiling, clad in their Sunday best. Perfectly grouped beneath the flattering light of a professional setup. Like something out of a catalogue.

"*Suburban American Family 101,*" Scrooge whispered. "*Get the picture?* I think Marley did. I think she had a hunch, but no proof. At HQ that night, just before she died, she'd been looking at the photographs..."

Scrooge whirled around to see Bobby giving instructions to the C.S.I. team, pointing out areas on which they should focus special attention. As they bent to the work of collecting samples, Oliver raised a camera and began snapping pictures.

"What do you think, Ollie?" Bobby asked, carefully stepping over some stray pieces of the dead parents which had fallen onto the carpet. "I'm running out of ideas. What the hell is this guy's problem? Why does Humbug want to ruin Christmas?"

Oliver spoke softly from behind his camera. "Who said that he does?"

"Sensationalistic nonsense," Scrooge said, recalling Oliver's words to him at the police station. "Humbug never called *himself* that. Just like my stupid nickname, his came from the press—*those vultures.*"

"What are you talking about" Bobby said, eyeing the photographer.

"You're the expert," Oliver shrugged, crouching so as to capture the scene from a different angle. "But it seems to me people like this ruined Christmas. Not to speak ill of the dead, but I mean come on, look at all that crap." He gestured toward the tree, the numerous large packages and boxes beneath it. "Is that what Christmas is about? What kind of person needs all of that to be happy?"

Oliver went to the wall of pictures and examined the central portrait. "I photograph people for a living, Detective—and not just dead people. Those smiles don't fool me for a second. This family, all of these families, they were miserable. And why? No reason for it. No reason but greed and pride."

"Both of which, I understand, are pretty serious sins." Bobby surveyed the scene again, as if looking for something he'd misplaced. "So you think Humbug is, what? Trying to punish people who don't celebrate Christmas in a way he thinks is proper? Or are the murders some kind of lesson for everyone else? A reminder to appreciate what they have."

"Nobody really appreciates anything until it's gone," Scrooge recited.

Oliver said, "People always treasure the wrong things the most." For a long moment, he continued staring at the photographs. "Do you realize that since the murders began there's been a major rise in extended family gatherings around Christmastime? Church functions and community parties, too. Safety in numbers, you see? Now nobody wants anybody to be alone. People are starting to care about each other again."

He turned from the wall and resumed photographing the room. "Listen to me, the bigtime philosopher, right? I think I'll stick to taking pictures, Detective, and leave plumbing the depths of troubled hearts to you."

"Sure," Bobby nodded. His face was directed at his notebook, but his eyes were on the photographer, his tone carefully neutral. "Back to work, then."

"You have to learn to see it from the other guy's perspective." Scrooge slammed a fist into his palm. "Goddamn right, Fred. This guy isn't out to destroy Christmas at all, he never was. We were looking for somebody trying to ruin the holiday and this sick son of a bitch was *celebrating* it."

He dashed over to Jack, who'd abandoned her place in the corner to loom over the mutilated parents, eyes alight with fascination and desire.

"I get it now, Jack. I see what we were missing all this time. Please, take me home so I can be there for Tim and Bobby. I want to help properly identify and arrest this psycho before he kills another family. I want to keep Tim from making a terrible mistake. There's work to be done and I've learned my lesson, I swear."

Jack unfastened the cloak from around her neck and draped it over their heads, sealing them in darkness. When she yanked it away, with the flourish of a stage magician revealing his beautiful assistant emerging from the box of swords alive and unharmed, Scrooge was momentarily blinded by the piercing light. He was battered by big flakes of snow that were oddly hard and sharp, collapsed into a stiff pile of the large white shapes, and found them warm to the touch. Far away, a voice boomed, "I don't even care anymore. Honestly, I don't."

The detective, recognizing the voice, loud though strangely muffled, as that of his own daughter, scrambled to his feet and ran toward it. He moved quickly around brightly painted plastic decorations—enormous candy canes stuck into the ground like fence posts and strangely short evergreens, their branches artfully bedecked with just the right amount of snow. All of it seemed *flat* somehow, unreal. Like the poorly constructed sets of an amateurish stage play or some cheap film shoot.

"It's been two weeks," Ellen said. Again, Scrooge heard her voice echoing all around him, but it was also dampened, as if she were speaking to him through a door (as she had so many times as a teenager). "I don't know why he didn't call me back and, frankly, I'm sick of all the drama. He knows my number, if he wants to call. Otherwise, I'm done with him."

Scrooge sprinted forward and ran into an invisible barrier that proved hard as concrete. The unexpected impact sent stars careening through his vision. Sprawled out in the rough, warm drifts of the not-snow, Scrooge blinked hard and tried to focus. Lying on his back, waiting for his vision to clear, he saw the shape of his daughter, gigantic but indistinct, blurry, as if seen through a sheet of warped plastic, and understood at last where exactly he'd been transported to.

A snow globe.

The detective brushed aside a flat plastic snowflake as it drifted toward his face and stood again. He had shrunk down to the size of an insect. The immense form of Ellen was stretched and distorted by the domed glass he was imprisoned beneath. He knew the larger space beyond to be her dorm room, having helped her move in just a few months ago, and Scrooge watched his daughter pacing in the cluttered space, phone pressed to one ear. He heard her saying that she wanted nothing more to do with him. Heard her saying he'd never called her back for Christmas. Saying that was nearly two weeks ago. Saying she *hated* him.

Face buried in his hands, Scrooge began to cry. "Please," he said, "give me another chance. I'm sorry that I let everyone down. I'm sorry!"

For a long time he knelt in the hard plastic and wept. Finally, his misery was interrupted by a darkening of the world, as if the sun itself had abruptly fled the sky. He looked up and saw Ellen had been replaced by the gigantic figure of the Ripper. Her irises glowed with queer pale light that made the black pupils even blacker and accented the gleaming spots of amber—sparks dancing off a bonfire. Twin alien suns dawning over a world in which Scrooge no longer had a place.

A white gloved hand the size of a mountain came rushing toward him and Scrooge screamed as he felt his plastic prison lifted skyward. The world shook violently and he was thrown about like a castaway tossed by angry waves—striking the ground, the clear dome, smacked by plastic flakes of snow and hurled into decorative set pieces. He was pummeled relentlessly, then came the sensation of falling as the Ripper opened her hand and released the toy.

Plummeting down while the floor sped to meet him, a collision imminent, unavoidable. Scrooge, bleeding from cuts and contusions, feeling a stab of pain from bones he was certain were broken, floated in the air surrounded by fake snow and closed his eyes. He waited for the impact, for a new and heretofore unimaginable level of agony to overtake him. For the start of cold and endless oblivion.

He waited to get exactly what he deserved.

Scrooge woke startled to find himself lying face down on the floor of his own apartment, fresh fireworks of pain exploding behind his eyes. Slowly, he forced himself onto his hands and knees, nearly toppled over, then righted himself. Scrooge brought a hand to his face and gently probed. He was, yet again, somehow seemingly unharmed.

Shakily on his feet at last, Scrooge surveyed his dismal home, taking careful note of the blackness outside the window, empty beer cans on the carpet, the shattered glass strewn about near the door—and the faceless corpse slumped in his recliner.

The cadaver's head was a nightmare of mutilation, all its features destroyed by the outward explosion of a gunshot from beneath where its chin used to be. On the floor beside his chair was a familiar pistol.

Scrooge had seen plenty of suicides in his time as a cop and knew instantly the fate of the miserable wretch before him. The truth of the story was evident in the wounds and the gore sprayed on the wall—and the carpet, and the ceiling. A ravenous cloud of flies swarmed every inch of the blood-soaked scene. Their buzzing in the small room was deafening, seeming almost to rattle the cheap, thin walls.

Clearly a man, the deceased wore an outfit identical to Scrooge's: black dress pants beneath a sleeveless white undershirt. His arms were adorned with tattoos just like Scrooge's, though less easily identifiable due to the body's advancing decomposition. Clearly, the man had been sitting in this apartment and rotting undisturbed for some time. Two weeks, maybe. Apparently, he wasn't missed.

Scrooge slowly took in the vision of his own putrefying carcass.

Obviously, this was to be his fate: tortured for all time by insane visions of monstrous, uncaught murderers from history, glimpsing moments from the lives of those people he'd abandoned and betrayed, and the occasional reminder that he was so utterly despised that nobody noticed when he finally put a bullet in his own head.

When the Ripper came slowly slithering out from behind the recliner, Scrooge was not surprised.

He watched in a state of numbness beyond shock, crippled by a degree of hopelessness beyond despair, as Jack slowly raised her skirts. Out spilled a mass of writhing tentacles, the slick flesh of each blacker than tar and dotted with large circular suction cups, all of them reaching greedily for his cadaver.

The snaking limbs latched onto Scrooge's dead body and began viciously tearing away pieces—flaps of skin, chunks of muscle, whole organs—raising the dripping prizes high as if in exaltation.

With elegantly gloved hands the Ripper lowered her scarlet scarf, revealing a small pink rosebud of a mouth. Even as Scrooge watched, transfixed, it bloomed, gaping impossibly wide to expose countless rings of razor-edged triangular shark's teeth spiraling down her gullet.

The tentacles carried their respective pieces of Scrooge to that awful orifice and shoved them inside to be gnawed, shredded, and swallowed. Streams of dark blood coursed down the Ripper's swanlike neck, splashing over the rounded tops of her heaving breasts, staining her previously immaculate skin and corset. The drips raining onto her squirming tentacles seemed to make them only more excited to eviscerate the dead policeman's putrid remains.

"I want to live."

Scrooge spoke the words so softly he was uncertain he'd actually said them. So, he said them again, louder.

"I want to live!"

The noise which erupted in response from the dank depths of the Ripper's throat was not quite a laugh. More like the blissful exclamation made by a snake contentedly coiling itself more tightly around something small and fuzzy. The cheerful clamoring of famished parasites penetrating the flesh of an unwary host. It was the delirious ecstasy of cancer as it metastasized.

Scrooge picked up the pistol and stood before the chair in which what little remained of his remains was being torn asunder by the world's most infamous psychopath. As another hunk of his flesh was sloppily chewed and swallowed by the Ripper, he raised the gun.

"Bon appétit, bitch."

Scrooge emptied the pistol. And in response, from some far off and unseen place, came a voice. Their tone was one of righteous fury, although the precise words were difficult to distinguish behind the anguished screams of the Ripper and roaring echo of gunfire in the tiny apartment.

Was it the voice of God? Scrooge wondered. *The will of the universe made audibly manifest?*

Scrooge lowered the weapon before screaming back, "I said I want to live!"

The voice returned, angrier now. "And I said shut the fuck up!"

Scrooge looked from the gun in his fist to the now-empty chair, it's worn black leather punctured by a cluster of bullet holes from which wisps of smoke rose as Scrooge considered them. His gaze roamed somewhat dazedly around his apartment and found the room was as it should be. The beer cans were there. The shattered whiskey bottle littered the carpet near the door. But there were no swarms of flies. No blood or bits of bone and brain coated the walls and ceiling, either. No faceless corpse was in evidence. No monstrous tentacled killer.

The angry voice of Scrooge's neighbor came through the meager wall again. "Was that a gun? You better quiet down or I swear to God I will call the police!"

"I am the police," Scrooge replied. "What's today?"

"Are you serious?"

"Please, what's today?"

"Today is Christmas fucking Day—well, barely. Jesus H. Christ, it's two o'clock in the goddamn morning, you noisy piece of shit!"

"Christmas fucking Day?!?"

Scrooge whooped and hollered and ran to the wall, banging his fists joyously upon it. "It's two o'clock in the goddamn morning on Christmas fucking Day! I'm not dead! I haven't missed it! The spirits, they managed the whole thing in one night—and of course they did! They can do whatever they like, right? Everyone knows that."

"Sure," the neighbor was exasperated, "everybody knows that. Now please, I'm begging you, go to sleep!"

"If only I could." Scrooge rushed to the recliner and began digging beneath the seat cushion, searching frantically for his phone, thinking it must have slipped from his pocket earlier that night. "But there's work to be done, sir. Lives are at stake—and souls, too! You said it, Marley, and you were absolutely right. Right as always! Just like old times. Ha!"

Scrooge snatched up his miraculously undamaged phone and for one truly unsettling moment, had no idea which call to make first. There were so many crises competing for his attention. Such a vast array of wrongs needing righted. A veritable hoard of amends to be made. But he forced himself to calm down, breathe more slowly, and allowed his pragmatic cop brain to take over.

Bobby answered on the second ring. "Detective Caine?" His voice was uncertain, cautious. "Are you okay?"

"Never better. Merry Christmas, by the way."

"Uh, sure. If I say 'you too' will you promise not to tear off my arm and beat me with it?"

"Ha! You're so funny, Bobby. I always meant to tell you that. How much I appreciate your humor."

"Thanks... I guess. What's up?"

"Are you at home? Is Lyla still there? We need to talk."

"She's back at my place. I couldn't sleep so I came down to HQ to go through the files again. Everybody's on standby just kind of waiting for, well, you know. The discovery. Hey, wait a minute, how did you know about me and Lyla?"

"I'm a detective, kid. Knowing stuff is sort of my job. Listen, I need you to check something for me. In the old cases, I need you to go back and look for any family portraits we took from the victims' houses. Who shot them? What company, I mean. And when they were taken, if you can find that."

Scrooge hurried to fill Bobby in on his theory—Marley's theory, actually. And after some initial incredulousness the young detective promised to get the facts and call right back.

True to his word, and in keeping with the talent which Scrooge had personally witnessed in him, Bobby did not take long. Scrooge barely had time to hurriedly shower, don his last clean suit, and reload his pistol before the phone rang.

As it turned out, Humbug's victims did have one thing in common: they'd all had family portraits done by the same small independent company. Each time, the pictures were taken no more than three months before Christmas, with copies probably intended to be sent to family and friends in time for the holiday.

The company was owned and operated by its lead (and sole) staff photographer: Oliver Drood.

"This doesn't actually mean he's the killer," Bobby said immediately.

"Not legally," Scrooge agreed.

"It just seems so impossible. I mean, we *know* the guy. We work with him every day. How can this be?"

"There will be time for those questions later."

"But he could already be inside the house of his next victims."

Bobby was again the eager student, desperate for some guidance or instruction from a trusted teacher. "He might be anywhere in the city. What are we going to do?"

Scrooge's memory flashed back to a certain dusty chess set. "You have to be able to see it from the other guy's perspective, kid. That's the only way to know what he's thinking. What he'll do next. And once you know that, you'll beat him every time."

"What the actual fuck are you talking about, Scrooge?"

"Don't call me that. Listen, you said the response team is on alert, right? Oliver's part of the team. So call him in."

"On what pretense?"

"The guy's a crime scene photographer, isn't he? Tell him there's been a crime. Tell him there's been a horrible murder—a whole family's been killed and you're sure it's Humbug. Say there was a card left at the scene and everything. He won't be able to resist coming right away to have a look."

"Okay," Bobby's voice held a smile. "That's good, it makes sense. But which family do I say is dead?"

"That's the easy part." Scrooge said, holstering his pistol. "Mine."

STAVE FIVE

A SEASON OF MIRACLES AND ATROCITIES (THE END OF IT)

"Bah!" said Scrooge. "Humbug!"

– Charles Dickens
A Christmas Carol

A flurry of emotions battled for dominance inside of Scrooge as he approached the house in which he'd once lived with his wife and daughter; the house where they'd gone on living without him. Excitement, vindication, apprehension, relief—so much of what happened in the past several hours seemed impossible, yet he never once doubted it all really had occurred.

And this, too, the imminent confrontation with the mad killer for whom he'd so relentlessly hunted, was really happening. The deserted suburban street and frosty early morning almost seemed to be holding their breath, as if in anticipation of the moment.

Located about twenty-five miles north of Seattle, connected by Interstate 5 as well as various bus and commuter train lines, the city of Everett was the most populous in Snohomish County. Although it boasted employment opportunities of its own, the city just as often served as a kind of bedroom community for those who worked in Seattle. Scrooge's former home sat on a relatively quiet street not far from a small naval station; a downright affordable location back when he'd purchased it many years ago as a young father eager to move his budding family away from the mean streets on which he'd seen so much violence.

A simple blue-white boxy affair with three floors, including a small attic, three bedrooms and garage. Once, it seemed like a long time ago now, Scrooge used to deliberately park his own car closer than necessary to his wife's to leave space for Marley's motorcycle to rest out of the elements on the occasions when she came over for dinner. Now, the flat gray doors were closed. All the lights were out. Of course, the occupants being in Hawaii, nobody was home; that was part of the plan. But where was Bobby?

Something is wrong.

They'd devised a simple attack: meet at the house and get the door open, turn the lights on, call for backup, and then summon Oliver. Scrooge felt certain Bobby would not have altered the plan without asking him first. There was no reason he shouldn't have beaten Scrooge to the house. No reason he shouldn't be standing out front, waiting to set their trap. Scrooge made his way cautiously up the short walkway to the porch. The front door was slightly ajar. He could detect no sounds beyond the gentle whispering of the frigid wind as it passed the house, unaware and uncaring of his situation.

Entering slowly, pistol drawn, Scrooge blinked hard, encouraging his eyes to adjust to the darkness quickly. Even as part of him could not help but register the changes his ex-wife had made to the interior—new furnishings arranged in alien configurations, a fresh coat of paint, and generous number of house plants—Scrooge eyed every shadowy corner for possible threats and went forward carefully, always expecting the worst.

He found Bobby in the kitchen.

The young detective was on the linoleum floor, trussed up and gagged, but conscious. He looked at Scrooge with large pleading eyes, but made no sound. A nasty wound on the right side of his forehead stood in evidence of how he'd come to arrive at such a predicament.

Ambush, Scrooge thought, *damn! The kid jumped the gun making the call and Oliver was closer than he guessed. And got here faster.*

Bobby rolled his eyes to the right, the direction of the house's back door, which led out onto a small deck that overlooked the rectangular yard Scrooge had spent so many bygone Saturdays watering and mowing. Scrooge nodded to show he understood and began backing out of the room, intent on circling around the house and trying to surprise Oliver. There was a small walkway between the property fence and backyard that Scrooge thought he could probably—

"Move and I'll kill him."

Oliver's voice came out of the darkness, somehow both familiar and strange, like a sound from a lingering nightmare. Gone was his jocular just-making-conversation tone, his casual Shop Talk voice replaced by this, something much colder. His true nature revealed.

"I have his own gun pointed right at his head."

Scrooge could almost imagine he heard the laughter of invisible spirits, but pushed the less-than-helpful fancies away for the moment. Instead, he looked directly into Bobby's wide and frightened eyes and said, "Go ahead."

Bobby's protests were indistinct through the gag, but vociferous enough to make his preference known.

"I mean, do you really think I care what happens to this douchebag?" Scrooge said. "The guy took my fucking job. You kill him, then I kill you, and I'll be a famous hero. You'll be lying in a morgue freezer faster than you can say *White Christmas* and I'll be sipping whiskey before breakfast. Sounds like a fine ending to me."

An interminable moment elapsed.

Then another.

Bobby struggled against his bonds.

Oliver remained perfectly silent.

Scrooge's grip tightened on the pistol.

"I chose a particularly special family this year," Oliver said at last. "So privileged, so completely spoiled, yet so miserable. I couldn't wait to teach them the true meaning of Christmas. And then, just as I was getting started, Detective Alwyn called. He recited quite a tale, but I heard the truth in his voice. He was so pathetically easy to surprise. As enjoyable as this diversion has proven, gentlemen,

I do hope to return to my new family soon. You see, I left them tied up in much the same way as Detective Alwyn here—except the floor on which they are lying is covered in a pool of gasoline. And I'm afraid the candles I left burning to set the proper mood are, well, rather short."

Scrooge tried to control his voice and keep out any trace of rage or frustration. He remembered Marley's code: *never let them see what you're thinking.*

"Okay," Scrooge said, "let's pretend I believe you're telling the truth about that—I don't, by the way. You're still identified, Oliver, and that's a fact. You're as good as caught even if you do somehow get away tonight. So let's work it out right here, right now. Tell me what you want."

The gentle humming of a familiar carol coming from the killer crouched in the dark made the flesh on Scrooge's arms crawl. "Peace on Earth," Oliver sang the words, "and good will to men."

"Admirable. But could you be a little more specific? Negotiations are about give and take. So come on, give me something."

"I see no reason I should negotiate with you, Detective. You have nothing I want."

"That's where you're wrong, Ollie. If you kill Bobby and I kill you then history will only have my word for why you did what you did. And if you leave it up to me, I'm going to make you out to be a real Grinch."

Oliver said nothing.

"I'll tell everybody you hated Christmas and wanted to ruin the holiday. You'll be a caricature by the time I'm done. A laughing stock forever."

"Nothing lasts forever."

"Maybe so, but this miserable trudge we call existence is longer than you think—*believe me*. You want to spend eternity as a legend or a joke?"

Oliver seemed to consider his options for a moment, humming to himself again. Finally, he said, "I think, perhaps, I'll take my chances."

Even as Scrooge prepared to dash forward, accepting the risks of abandoning his position of cover, every window in the house exploded in a flash of light so blindingly brilliant that Scrooge sincerely believed for a second that Oliver somehow had snuck around behind him and shot him in the head.

But no, he was not dead.

Scrooge's vision cleared and the light remained, streaming into the house with the intensity of the sun, but none of the warmth. Outside arose the clatter of helicopter blades and a commanding amplified voice filled the room, announcing the presence of the Seattle Police Department. The house was surrounded, they said. Everyone inside was ordered to exit the domicile immediately, hands raised over their heads.

"I just thought of another reason for you to negotiate," Scrooge shouted to be heard above the noise. "Seems you weren't the only call my premature young colleague made tonight!"

No response.

Scrooge inched forward into the kitchen.

Bobby—bound and wounded, perhaps, but still an experienced combat veteran—rolled to the right, accidentally smashing his head into the counter, but escaping just as Oliver fired the pistol.

A bullet exploded into the floor at the exact spot where he'd been a second before. Insanely, Scrooge's mind went briefly to his ex-wife, how he might explain the damage to her kitchen. *She is* not *going to like that,* he thought, raising his pistol with both hands.

Again, the amplified voice ordered everyone to exit the domicile immediately. The cacophony of sirens and chopper blades was deafening.

Had they heard the gunshot?

Did they understand what was happening inside?

Having allowed himself to become distracted, Scrooge was outdrawn. Oliver's second shot, when it struck Scrooge in the fleshy part of his upper left arm, did not feel as the detective always expected. Despite the notoriously brutal nature of his long and storied career as a policeman, his lack of hesitation when it came to the use of force, throughout countless aggressive interrogations and many physical altercations, Detective Stewart Caine had never been shot before.

It hurt.

A lot.

Way more than he thought it would.

The pistol fell from his hand as Scrooge stumbled and went down to one knee, feeling the hot gush of blood seeping from his wound, somehow hearing (or imagining he could hear) it spatter on the floor.

Well, he thought, laughing weakly, *at least I won't be around to answer for this mess.*

Oliver snatched up Scrooge's gun and tossed it away, all the while still brandishing Bobby's pistol. He was sweating profusely and had to push his glasses up on his nose more than once.

"What's so funny?"

"I was just thinking how my wife is going react when she sees what you did to her kitchen. You might do better in prison, Ollie. I know that woman. Seriously, think it over."

Oliver grabbed hold of Bobby and dragged him over to lie closer to Scrooge, then crouched, eyes behind his thick lenses once again, as when contemplating his gory photos, alight with anticipation.

Laying a finger aside of his nose, Oliver pushed up his glasses, while the corners of his mouth inched toward his eyes in what seemed a nearly painfully big smile. "I like you, Detective. I always did. Before your brothers in arms come crashing in here to put an end to our time together, I just wanted you to know that."

Leveled with his face, the pistol's barrel was like a tunnel—a long dark tunnel into whose depths Scrooge stared with weary resignation. "God bless us," he said, "everyone."

Oliver let loose a sharp bark of laughter. "To all a good night, Scrooge."

"Humbug."

"Don't call me that."

Bobby's feet, tied together at the ankles, lashed out as one, struck Oliver unawares in the hip and sent him sprawling. Although he managed to keep hold of the pistol, his glasses skidded away and out of reach.

Scrooge leapt forward, punching Oliver in the face with his un-injured arm. The impact connected with a resounding *crack!* that could be heard even above the commotion outside. He grabbed Oliver's wrist and twisted until the gun fell away. They wrestled for a moment, but the photographer, though smaller and not nearly as strong, regained the advantage when he dug his fingers into Scrooge's gunshot wound and squeezed.

The detective screamed and his vision went black as he nearly lost consciousness from the influx of additional pain. But he managed, at the last second, to slightly redirect himself as he collapsed and brought his forearm down across Oliver's throat with all his remaining might. He used his own not-inconsiderable weight and the force of gravity itself to pinch the murderer's throat shut.

A terrible straining noise escaped from Oliver's gaping mouth, the corners of which hadn't lowered a bit, as if he were still enjoying this new turn of events, even now. Scrooge pressed down harder, his head full of voices.

"Do it," cooed the Butcher. "He deserves it."

"*You deserve it,*" whispered Zodiac. "*Think how good it will feel. Another definition of 'present' is gift. Treat yourself, Detective.*"

Jack's eyes glittered in Scrooge's mind, full of unspoken promises and wondrous revelations. Glad tidings. Peace on Earth. Comfort and joy.

Scrooge pulled back, just a little. "Tell me," he whispered, nose barely an inch from Oliver's, "where is the next family? Tell me or I swear I'll break your neck. There will be no trial. No swaggering for the cameras. No books. No documentary series. You won't live to enjoy a second of your precious infamy unless you give me an address right now!"

And he did.

Looking up into the eyes of a man who so clearly longed to murder him, Oliver took the choice he'd never offered his own victims and elected to live. Hissing and rasping with the effort, Humbug confessed the location of his latest family.

"Please," he groaned, "don't...."

"You'll live, you twisted little shit. Don't worry, you're going to be arrested and go to trial and be held accountable for what you did."

At the sound of doors being broken down, the thunderous storm of SWAT team boots stampeding into the house, Scrooge took his arm away from Oliver's neck and said to the gasping red-faced serial killer, "Merry Christmas, motherfucker."

Then he punched him one more time.

The paramedics found Scrooge a less than cooperative patient, who, despite their repeated insistence, refused to be transported to the hospital.

A glorified field dressing and some basic pain meds were the most he'd accept, sitting in the back of an ambulance outside his ex-wife's house as the SWAT team secured the scene and he and Bobby gave preliminary statements to the brass. All of his so-called superiors, beyond excited to give him the boot less than a day before, now swarmed Scrooge with praise.

Uniformed cops, meanwhile, hurried to unroll crime scene tape and tried to keep reporters, camera crews, and nosy neighbors a discrete distance away as Oliver Drood was hastened into the back of a squad car and taken to headquarters. His neck was badly bruised, and the blood vessels which exploded in his eyes did nothing to improve his appearance, but the smile never once left the man's face.

Bobby leaned against the ambulance with an icepack held against his head. "I'm so, so sorry, Detective."

"I know," Scrooge said.

"No, I feel really terrible. The whole thing, I almost screwed it all up just because I so badly wanted to be the guy who got him."

"I get it."

"But it was selfish."

"Yes."

"It was stupid."

"Yes."

"It almost got us both killed."

"That too."

"Can you ever forgive me?" Bobby asked.

"Sure, kid. No problem."

"I'm being serious."

"So am I. A good friend of mine, a cop much smarter than both of us, and who fell into the exact same trap you did, recently reminded me there's more to life than being the smartest person in the room. And I've got bigger, more important things to worry about than headlines and medals. So do you, I bet. Think it over. That pretty paramedic likes you just fine the way you are. And so do I. Merry Christmas, Bobby."

"Merry Christmas, Stewart."

Scrooge sat inside the ambulance grinding his teeth and cracking his knuckles. The waiting seemed endless. His phone rang twice, but Scrooge, recognizing the number, ignored it. The chief could wait, whether she liked it or not. He was, technically speaking, not even at work at the moment, not officially. The realization made him laugh out loud.

At last they were informed that a team of cops had found the family Oliver left to burn, mostly unharmed. Immediately, Bobby's phone rang.

"Hello? Yes, Chief Woodard. Merry Christmas to you, too. So we were just told. That's correct, the photographer. Yes, he's in custody now."

Scrooge got out of the ambulance, brushing past the flustered paramedics and beaming brass and curious onlookers, stalking off in the direction of his car, leaving the younger man scurrying to follow.

"Uh, Detective?" Bobby said. "The chief would like a word with you."

"It's your case, kid. You deal with her."

Bobby had a quick, hushed exchange with Seattle's top cop. "I'm sorry, but she's insisting. You'll have to talk to her eventually. You know that, right?"

"Yeah, sure." Scrooge stopped at his rust-red Ford Taurus and searched for his keys. "I'm thinking the first of the year sounds good. Please remind the chief I'm on a leave of absence—with pay, of course."

"I don't understand," Bobby stammered, uncomprehending. "You can't just... Where the hell are you going?"

"Sorry." Scrooge got behind the wheel and reached to close the door. "But there's one more name on this fat old man's naughty list."

The lock on Jasper Sikes' door was a joke. Scrooge, tired as he was, destroyed it with just one kick. None of the junkies and scoundrels sleeping in the living room, who'd been soundly dreaming their drunken, stoned dreams, hesitated to flee when given the chance. In the bedroom, Scrooge found Jasper similarly comatose and slapped him awake.

"I know you—you're that cop they talk about on TV all the time!" A thoroughbred criminal with years of experience, Jasper quickly leapt to his feet, immediately understanding the situation. "What the hell are you doing here, Scrooge?"

"Don't call me that."

Jasper was saying things like, "Unlawful entry...lack of probable cause...inadmissible in court—"

"Shut up." The depth of anger in Scrooge's voice, his clearly disheveled appearance, and the fact he'd yet to show a badge, silenced Jasper instantly. Whatever this was, it obviously wasn't a raid. "Merry Christmas, Jasper."

"Fuck you."

Scrooge administered another slap, this one hard enough to knock Jasper back into his bed.

"Damn," Scrooge said, "I didn't want to do that. Why'd you make me do that? Come on, try again. I said 'Merry Christmas, Jasper.' Now here's the part where you say it to me."

Wiping his bloody lip with the back of one hand, Jasper mumbled something close enough.

"I used to hate this holiday," Scrooge said. "I mean really, truly despise it. But I'm trying to be a better person. Call it an early New Year's resolution, but I'm endeavoring to keep the spirit of the season in my heart even when dealing with a piece of shit like you. There was a time I'd only just be warming up now for the ass kicking to come. You see, I know all about your little delivery service with the boy next door. But with it being Christmas, and me turning over a new leaf, so to speak, I thought rather than a swiftly broken spine, today, I'd bring you a gift instead. Are you listening, Jasper?"

The dealer nodded.

Forty-eight hours. That was the present Scrooge gave to Jasper: two whole days to pack his things and get out of town, no questions asked.

"Never mind about your parole officer, I'll take care of him. It's a great big, beautiful country out there, Jasper, and full of places where a smart scumbag like you could earn a handsome living. Because, you see, I plan on spending a lot more time in this neighborhood. And although I have every intention of sticking to my goal of being a less violent person, the more often I have to look at your stupid ugly mug, the harder that's going to be. I'm only human, Jasper. And we all struggle. You hearing me?"

Jasper nodded again, the side of his face already starting to darken and swell.

"Excellent! I'm glad we had this chat." Scrooge paused in the bedroom doorway and said, without turning, "And stay away from that girl, Clarissa. She's way too young for you, Jasper. And that's extra trouble you don't need right now, wouldn't you agree?"

The look on Jasper's bruised face was difficult to describe. There was anger to be seen there, although it was tightly controlled. A flicker of fear moved through his eyes, too, but only for a second. Mostly, he just looked stunned. Utterly perplexed. Maybe even a little amazed.

He'd only just met that girl a few days ago.

The noisy commotion of people taking flight from Jasper's home had roused his neighbors and the lights of several adjacent houses were on when Scrooge stepped back into the cold darkness of the predawn Christmas morning.

Not exactly unaccustomed to suspicious goings-on at the Sikes home, somebody—possibly more than one person—had already called the police. Faintly, Scrooge heard sirens in the distance. Across the street, Belle stood in her yard, wrapped in a heavy blanket, long hair loose and tousled. Her face was stern, but the tone in which she shouted, her words steaming in the chilly air, was friendly.

"You're late!"

Scrooge plodded over, his arm on fire, all the muscles and joints in his body feeling every single day of his age. "Sorry," he said. "I got stuck at work."

"I know." Belle's hand emerged from the folds of the blanket holding her phone. "It's online already. Tim saw it first and told me. You're trending, apparently, for whatever that's worth. Did you really catch Humbug?"

"I helped," Scrooge stopped just out of arm's reach and they stood regarding each other for a long moment. "Where's Tim?"

"Inside, watching the news on TV. It's funny, he told me that he wouldn't go back to bed tonight until you showed up. I told him you probably weren't coming, but he insisted you would. He's proud of you, you know. And I think he's more excited than anyone else in Seattle about what you did tonight. But I'm confused because I thought you were off the case? What happened to your drunken vacation plans and staying home alone tonight?"

"Call it volunteer work. People do that at Christmastime, right?"

"People do, yes. But you don't."

"Maybe I'm trying new things." The sirens were growing louder. "Next, I thought I might try apologizing."

Belle nodded as she turned and walked back into the house. "Can you come and try it inside, please? I'm freezing my ass off out here."

"I certainly wouldn't want to see anything bad happen to that ass." Scrooge had only just moved to follow when his phone rang. A distinctive ringtone, and different from the one he'd assigned the chief. This one, he'd only assigned to one person. And he knew it right away.

"It's Ellen," he said. "I've kind of been waiting for this."

Belle was a woman expertly familiar with performative affection, knew the real thing when she saw it, and wasn't afraid to walk away when she didn't. Now, she regarded Scrooge with the same appraising eye she used to select promising antiques. There was something of value there, she seemed to be thinking. Something worthwhile to keep.

"We've got nothing but time," she said. "I'll go tell Tim he was right and warm up some food for you."

"Thanks, Belle. I'll be right in."

His daughter was shouting before Scrooge could say a word.

"Oh my god, Dad, the internet is blowing up! Everybody is talking about how you caught Humbug. Are you okay? What happened? Was there really a shootout at our house? Mom is going to be soooo pissed! How'd you figure it out?"

"Merry Christmas, Ellen."

"What? Yeah, sure. Merry Christmas, Dad.

"How's Hawaii?"

"It's fine, I guess."

"Are you getting along with—what's his name again? Terry? Larry?"

"Harry? How did you know about Mom's new boyfriend?"

"Why are people surprised when I know stuff? I'm a detective, honey, it's my job."

"Okay, whatever. Sorry. Now will you please tell me how you knew who Humbug was? It's so cool, Dad. You finally got the guy!"

"I actually had some help."

"Is that right?"

"You see, earlier tonight I was visited by three spirits. They were the Ghosts of Christmas Past, Present—"

Ellen made a loud gagging sound. "Come on, Dad! Be serious, please. We had to read that book for class—it was soooo boring! I always hated that corny Dickens crap."

"Yeah, I know."

Red and blue lights flashed at the end of the block. Scrooge saw Jasper watching through a window in the house across the street, ducking quickly out of sight as their eyes met. From somewhere far away he heard the sound of a motorcycle speeding off to parts unknown, imagined the faint tinkling of chains, and Scrooge smiled.

"I used to feel the same way."

ABOUT THE AUTHOR

Luciano Marano is an award-winning author, journalist, and photographer.

Born at a now defunct military base in Central America, he grew up in rural Western Pennsylvania before completing a five-year enlistment in the U.S. Navy, where he served as a Mass Communication Specialist. Later, he received a BFA in commercial photography from a for-profit art school that no longer exists.

He is the author of the werewolf novella trilogy *The Ambush Moon Cycle* (Raven Tale Publishing) and numerous works of short fiction appearing in anthologies such as *Year's Best Hardcore Horror* and *The Best New Weird Horror*, among others, as well as *Nightscript, PseudoPod, Chthonic Matter Quarterly*, and *Chilling Tales for Dark Nights.*

His written and photographic reporting has earned a number of industry accolades, and he was twice named a Feature Writer of the Year by the Washington Newspaper Publishers Association.

He resides near Seattle with his wife.

THE END?

Not if you want to dive into more of Crystal Lake Publishing's Tales from the Darkest Depths!

Check out our amazing website and online store or download our latest catalog here.

We always have great new projects and content on the website to dive into, as well as a newsletter, behind the scenes options, social media platforms, our own dark fiction shared-world series and our very own webstore. Our webstore even has categories specifically for KU books, non-fiction, anthologies, and of course more novels and novellas.

Readers...

Thank you for reading *Humbug*. We hope you enjoyed this novella. If you have a moment, please review *Humbug* at the store where you bought it.

Help other readers by telling them why you enjoyed this book. No need to write an in-depth discussion. Even a single sentence will be greatly appreciated. Reviews go a long way to helping a book sell, and is great for an author's career. It'll also help us to continue publishing quality books.

Thank you again for taking the time to journey with Crystal Lake Publishing.

You will find links to all our social media platforms on our Linktree page.
https://linktr.ee/CrystalLakePublishing

Follow us on Amazon:

MISSION STATEMENT

Since its founding in August 2012, Crystal Lake has quickly become one of the world's leading publishers of Dark Fiction and Horror books. In 2023, Crystal Lake officially transitioned into an entertainment company, joining several other divisions, genres, and imprints, including Torrid Waters, Crystal Lake Comics, Crystal Lake Games, Crystal Lake Kids, and many more.

While we strive to present only the highest quality fiction and entertainment, we also endeavour to support authors along their writing journey. We offer our time and experience in non-fiction projects, as well as author mentoring and services, at competitive prices.

With several Bram Stoker Award wins and many other wins and nominations (including the HWA's Specialty Press Award), Crystal Lake Publishing puts integrity, honor, and respect at the forefront of our publishing operations.

We strive for each book and outreach program we spearhead to not only entertain and touch or comment on issues that affect our readers, but also to strengthen and support the Dark Fiction field and its authors.

Not only do we find and publish authors we believe are destined for greatness, but we strive to work with men and women who endeavour to be decent human beings who care more for others than themselves, while still being hard working, driven, and passionate artists and storytellers.

Crystal Lake Publishing is and will always be a beacon of what passion and dedication, combined with overwhelming teamwork and respect, can accomplish. We endeavour to know each and every one of our readers, while building personal relationships with our authors, reviewers, bloggers, podcasters, bookstores, and libraries.

We will be as trustworthy, forthright, and transparent as any business can be, while also keeping most of the headaches away from our authors, since it's our job to solve the problems so they can stay in a creative mind. Which of course also means paying our authors.

We do not just publish books, we present to you worlds within your world, doors within your mind, from talented authors who sacrifice so much for a moment of your time.

There are some amazing small presses out there, and through collaboration and open forums we will continue to support other presses in the goal of helping authors and showing the world what quality small presses are capable of accomplishing. No one wins when a small press goes down, so we will always be there to support hardworking, legitimate presses and their authors. We don't see Crystal Lake as the best press out there, but we will always strive to be the best, strive to be the most interactive and grateful, and even blessed press around. No matter what happens over time, we will also take our mission very seriously while appreciating where we are and enjoying the journey.

What do we offer our authors that they can't do for themselves through self-publishing?

We are big supporters of self-publishing (especially hybrid publishing), if done with care, patience, and planning. However, not every author has the time or inclination to do market research, advertise, and set up book launch strategies. Although a lot of authors are successful in doing it all, strong small presses will always be there for the authors who just want to do what they do best: write.

What we offer is experience, industry knowledge, contacts and trust built up over years. And due to our strong brand and trusting fanbase, every Crystal Lake Publishing book comes with weight of respect. In time our fans begin to trust our judgment and will try a new author purely based on our support of said author.

With each launch we strive to fine-tune our approach, learn from our mistakes, and increase our reach. We continue to assure our authors that we're here for them and that we'll carry the weight of the launch and dealing with third parties while they focus on their strengths—be it writing, interviews, blogs, signings, etc.

We also offer several mentoring packages to authors that include knowledge and skills they can use in both traditional and self-publishing endeavours.

We look forward to launching many new careers.

This is what we believe in. What we stand for. This will be our legacy.

Welcome to Crystal Lake Publishing—Where Stories Come Alive!

Printed in Dunstable, United Kingdom